ANGELA D. SHELTON

Downfall

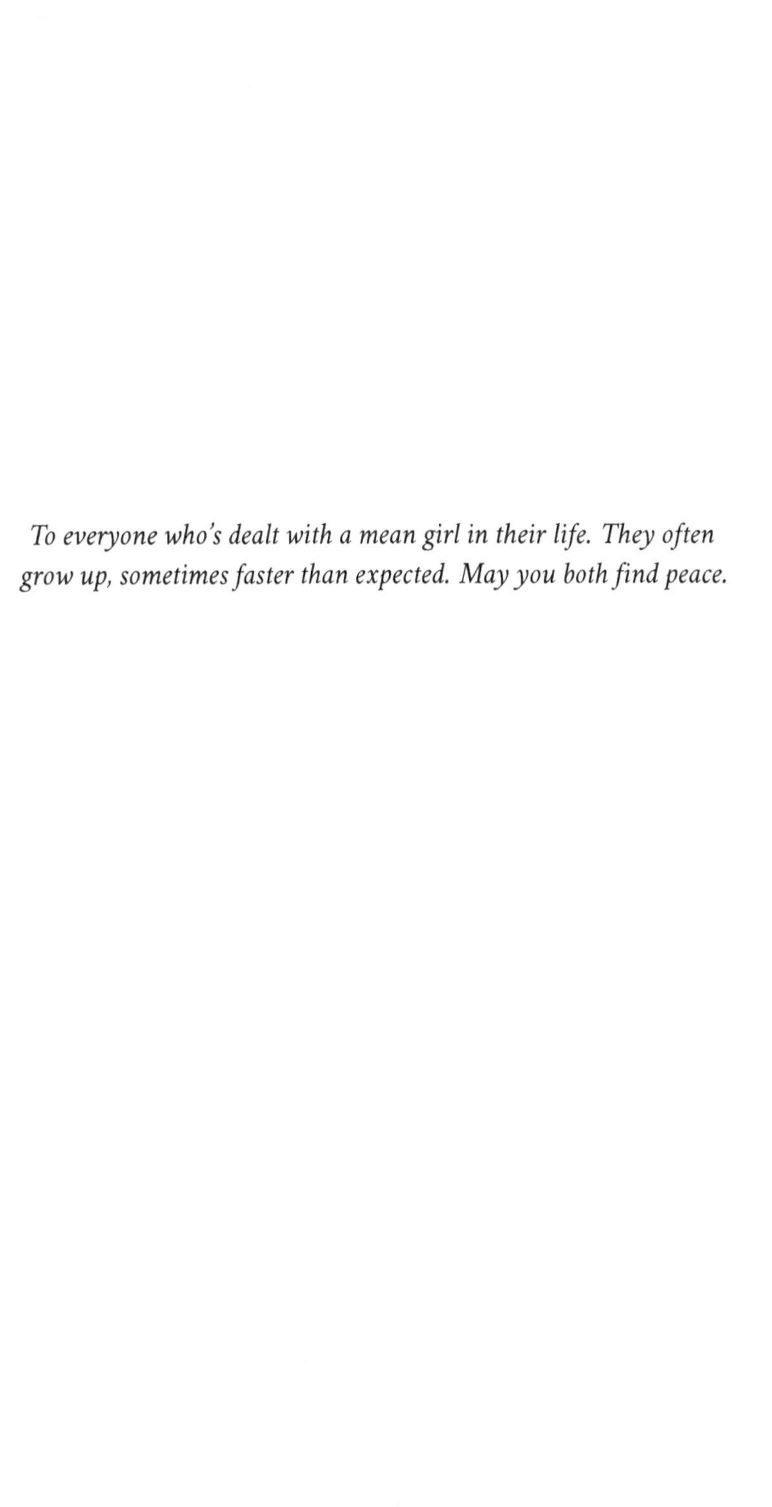

To everyone who's dealt with a mean girl in their life. They often grow up, sometimes faster than expected. May you both find peace.

Contents

1

Chapter One

Mom didn't understand. This wasn't 1995 anymore. Thirteen-year-old Lizzy Tilbrook stuffed the black T-shirt with a sparkly red I Dare You emblazoned across the chest into her book bag. She'd change back into it at school, where Mom couldn't monitor her every move. As she pulled on a different top, one Mom would say was more appropriate, her frustration escalated. Why did Mom want to control her every move?

She wasn't a little kid anymore.

A quick peek in the dresser mirror revealed her freckled face. Great. Her light-blond curls were out of control. Static cling was her reward for pulling the shirt on in haste. She tamped her hair back into place, careful not to excite the tresses into a frizz. When your hair was naturally curly, it could go from cute to crazy faster than a rapper could spit out a phrase. Good enough.

A pair of leggings rested on the bag's bottom. No way would she have gotten past her parents with the shirt/legging combo she'd planned to wear, but why did Mom have to be so militant about the shirt? What was the problem with a stupid saying on it, anyway? It was funny.

How many times had she and Mom argued over the school dress code? These days, it seemed like an ongoing war in which this was just the latest skirmish. A battle she'd lost, unfortunately. Someday, her parents' control wouldn't keep her from expressing herself. She couldn't wait.

She had to hurry to avoid being late. Walking into class after the first bell had rung was the worst. Mr. Evans always made a huge deal out of anyone being tardy, and she needed time to change before she went to his classroom.

She darted through the house, back to the kitchen where Mom packed her laptop back into her own rolling bag. "Gotta go, Mom. We're going to be late. I told you I didn't have time to change."

Mom tilted her head to the side, mouth twisted into her "whatever" look. "If you'd dressed appropriately in the first place, you wouldn't have to change your clothes. Don't blame me for your errors in judgment."

Errors in judgment. Who said that these days? And her mother had no fashion sense whatsoever. Most of the girls wore sexy leggings and clingy tops at school. If everyone was wearing them, why couldn't she? Mom was going to ruin her chances of becoming homecoming queen her senior year. Yes, it was a long way off, but you had to plan years in advance when you had goals. Being in the right crowd, running with the popular girls, and having the eyes of the trendy boys was critical to the mission.

"Let's just go." She moaned those last words, which caused Mom's eyes to narrow even further.

"Humph." Mom popped her lunch bag onto the rolling bag.

She paused and looked at Lizzy's book bag, then reached over and patted it on the bottom. "Are you carrying clothes in your bag?"

Shoot. How did she know? Think fast. "I have phys ed at school. Remember?"

It wasn't a lie—precisely. She had gym class. Just not today. And she'd leave it up to Mom to connect the dots that she hadn't said the clothes were workout wear.

Mom crossed her arms over her chest. "Let's see those shorts then."

Busted.

Lizzy's shoulders drooped as she yanked the zipper open and dragged out the contraband shirt.

Mom's right eyebrow lifted toward her hairline. "What else?"

No! Not the pants too.

Lizzy reached back into her pack, wiggled out the tiny sparkling leggings with ruching on the rear, then placed the clothes in her mother's outstretched hand.

As her mother inspected the clothing, Lizzy reclosed her bag with a defeated huff. "Happy now?"

The fiery look on her mother's face revealed anything *but* joy. "Where did you even get pants like this? What would your father say if he saw you wearing it? I can't even imagine."

No, she probably couldn't. How could any adult understand the current fashion trends? Look at her, dressed like a corporate automaton in her gray suit jacket and slacks. Lizzy didn't want to end up like that. The clipped-on badge Mom wore declared she was owned by a corporation. The company controlled what she wore, what hours she worked, and even what color her hair could be. Lizzy would never let that happen to her.

She glared right back. "You ruin everything. Now I'm going

to look like a dork at school all day. All the girls are wearing clothes like that. I'm going to be the only one who isn't. Do you know how that will make me feel?"

Mom headed toward the door, indicating the conversation would only continue if Lizzy followed. "I'm going to say to you the same thing my mom always said to me. If your friends all jumped off a bridge, would you follow?"

Flames washed over her like a volcano had just erupted inside her head. "Who even says that anymore, Mom? You are so ancient."

They climbed into Mom's Lexus LC 500, her birthday gift to herself this past spring. Rather than pull up in the pretentious thing, Lizzy preferred Mom drop her off a block away from the school, so her friends didn't see her in it.

"Well, you can contemplate all the terrible ways of your dear old mother every night this week because you're grounded, young lady."

Those flames now burned hot in her stomach. "Grounded? For wanting to express my personal style instead of becoming a clone?"

Mom huffed. "Keep it up. We can make it two. Then how many of your friends' invitations will you have to turn down?"

Mom pushed the button to start the car and backed out of the garage.

That was it. Lizzy was beat. Time to play dead and let her mom win. But she didn't have to be happy about it. Her silent protest would last all week so Mom and Dad both knew they could control her movements, but not her mind. They could never turn her into an android, doing everyone's bidding. They couldn't buy her with all the stuff they worked long hours to accumulate. Some things in life money couldn't provide.

She dug into the front pocket of her book bag for her face mask and covered her mouth and nose. The plain black covering protecting her from the virus was as dark as she felt inside. Little did Mom know. She had another mask hidden in a small zipper pocket. That one would be on her face as soon as she stepped inside the school walls. It sparkled with the rhinestone words *Wild Child*.

She was so tired of the virus and the constant changes and interruptions. Masks—no masks. In-school—remote learning. After-school activities on—canceled. She wanted her life back the way it was supposed to be. Football games with bleachers filled to maximum capacity, parties after the games, and no face-smothering coverings.

She knew several people who'd contracted the virus, and only a few had gotten sick worse than the normal flu bug. Why did everyone make a big deal out of it?

The only bonus she could come up with was the ability to hide behind the mask. Her parents were always harping on her about her "attitude." They loved to interpret her facial reactions as "disrespectful." Of course, she'd need a ski mask to hide her eye expressions, but she'd gotten the eye rolls under control. The covering allowed her to smirk at will, though—her saving grace.

Mom parked at the pharmacy, their normal drop-off point, and Lizzy opened her car door to exit.

"Have a good day." Mom practically sang the words as if the morning had been this bright, cheery experience, instead of the latest battle in their back-and-forth conflict.

But Lizzy didn't dare ignore the goodbye. "Yeah, right. Bye."

Closing the car door behind her was like closing a jail door with a work privilege release. She could go to school all day, but she'd be right back in prison soon after. What a life. Why couldn't she have chill parents like her best friend, Ava Russo? They never seemed to care what she wore to school—if only.

Lizzy slogged through the trail of students headed for their classrooms. In her homeroom, Ava waited in their usual spot, at the far rear corner of desks. Being back with her felt good.

"Did you see what Rachael Marshall wore this morning?" Ava loved to gossip.

"Knowing her, probably some knockoff Michael Kors." Lizzy pulled out a compact and applied some eyeliner she kept hidden in her backpack.

"If only." Ava giggled. "She's wearing sweatpants. To school. Can you believe it? And it's not like they're PINK or American Eagle."

Ava's Italian heritage gave her golden skin as well as dark hair that would be luxurious if she let it grow out. But Lizzy always insisted it looked cuter short. No need to add more competition for the guys' attention. And Ava would do anything Lizzy asked to hang with the popular kids.

After homeroom, they stopped at their lockers. Lizzy looked up and down the hallway, making sure there wasn't someone she needed to greet or connect with. Keeping up the pretense of being the friendliest girl in school was important. After all, you don't win the class president race unless every popular student in your grade thinks you're their BFF.

As she closed her locker and twisted the knob to relock it, Michael Flintwood strolled toward them. She cocked her hip to one side.

"Morning, Michael." The mask hid her plastered-on smile, but surely, it reached her eyes. Guys always wanted to be paid attention to. "You ready for your party this weekend?"

He paused. One thumb hooked in the pocket of his blue jeans while the other held the strap of the book bag slung over one shoulder.

Michael's older brother, Sean, was the captain of the high school football team. Whenever their parents were out of town, Sean threw an enormous party. He allowed Michael to invite some of his friends. Getting an invitation was a badge of honor. Even though Mom grounded her, Lizzy needed him to *want* her there.

"Yeah. Sean said I can only invite a dozen people, though. Said the beer costs too much." A shy-guy grin crept over his face, and he shuffled his sneakers. "I'd love it if you'd be one of my twelve."

Perfect. Now, even if she couldn't go, everyone would know she'd been on the invite list.

Bragging rights was all that mattered.

She changed the smile into a pout. It wasn't nearly as effective with the mask on, but even Michael had to get the gist.

"Sure wish I could. Got busted this morning, so I'm grounded for a week." She knew to not let the pout stay too long. No guy wanted to be with a Debbie Downer. The smile returned to her face, and she hoped her eyes were sparkling. "I can't wait for the next one, though. Rain check?"

The disappointment crumpling his masked face was priceless. "Yeah, next time. Well, gotta get to class. Later."

The last thing Lizzy needed was a boyfriend, but if she ever wanted one, Michael would be an obvious target. But a guy would just slow her down, and she had goals to reach. As he sauntered off, Ava watched him for the length of the hallway.

She'd had a crush on him since kindergarten. Silly.

"Earth to Ava." Lizzy jabbed her friend in the ribs. "We need to get those posters up in the hallways after school today. Did you get them done last night?"

Ava gazed back at Lizzy, confusion crinkling her eyes. Then those eyes widened. "Oh! Of course, you know I wouldn't forget. Red and black, just like you asked for. They're in my locker. Everyone will want to vote for you."

Her supposed best friend was great at the artsy stuff. They'd look fantastic. Ava had more talent in her pinkie than Lizzy had in her entire body. But that was all right by her. She didn't need to be artistic. She just needed to know where to get the resource.

She intended to be a lawyer by twenty-four. She'd fight for the rights of those who had no voice. Anticorporate, antiestablishment, and antidrudgery. Those would be her mottos.

She might be the only big-time lawyer in Atlanta with a streak of purple hair, but people would respect her because she'd beat the big-city firms every time with her extraordinary talent.

But it all started with winning the class president race. Mom always said you had to plan for the long haul and no one was going to help you like you can help yourself.

Mom came from a poor background. She loved to tell stories about growing up as a family of farmers who barely kept food on their table. She'd had to work a full-time job and take night classes to put herself through school. Even then, the huge student loan debt dogged her for years. Now, she was one of the top accountants at her CPA firm. A partner.

Mom pulled in the big bucks and told Lizzy she could go to any college she wanted to, though Mom pushed for the University of Georgia, her alma mater. But Lizzy had her eyes on Yale. Just the school's name would get her through doors, and her parents could afford it. So why not have the best?

"I wasn't kidding about being grounded. We need to get the signs up right after the last bell."

Ava shifted her book bag to the opposite shoulder. "I can finish it for you if you need to get home."

Of course she would. Ava always did whatever Lizzy needed. One step ahead of the need, usually. That's what best friends were for. At least Lizzy let Ava believe she was her best friend. She didn't really need anyone, not even a BFF.

Friendship had a time and place, and Ava filled that role. But Lizzy was a solid rock of determination. No one would stand in the way of her success.

This semester, she'd win class president. Then she'd be a shoo-in for the role every year until she was eligible for the student body president. That would look fantastic on her Yale application.

Success wasn't so hard when you had a plan. And hers was solid.

2

Chapter Two

Lizzy sat down for dinner between her parents, who resided at opposite ends of the long oak table. One may or may not classify their meals as homemade. Mom never had time to cook but insisted on picking up prepackaged meals from the local restaurant, Minnie's Place, and reheating them.

"Ms. Minnie said the collard greens are this year's first harvest." Mom spooned a generous serving onto Lizzy's plate. "And you know she makes the best in town."

Nice try, Mom, on getting me to eat the dreaded greens. Normally, Mom waited until Lizzy'd eaten all the carbs on her plate before nagging about the nonstarchy vegetables. Tonight, though, Mom was starting early. Great.

Lizzy accepted the plate of grilled chicken, pinto beans, and collards. Cornbread was in a basket, and she took a slab to nibble.

"I got the posters up today. Voting is Friday, so I figured I could give out the cookies on Thursday."

"Excellent." Mom spooned food onto Dad's plate. "I ordered

ten dozen fresh baked and individually wrapped from Ms. Minnie. We can pick them up after school on Wednesday. I'll bring home labels so you can put your campaign slogan on them. They're chocolate chip. No one turns down Ms. Minnie's chocolate chip cookies."

The cookies would be a hit, especially with the boys. It appeared the guys could eat three thousand calories a day and never gain an ounce. So not fair. Most likely, some cookies given to the girls in class would end up with the guys, but what mattered was having her name out there and attached to the treats.

"Ava said she'd help design the label so the graphics match up to the posters she hung today. The cookies will cement the deal." Lizzy bit into her piece of cornbread.

"Wait, what?" Dad's thick golden-brown eyebrows slanted downward. "Are you trying to bribe the student body into voting for you?"

She rolled her eyes. He was so straitlaced. Mom said that's why he'd never made it to the executive level at his construction company. He never worked the crowd or did favors for upper management.

According to Mom, if you wanted to win, you had to grease the wheels. The students expected bribery. And what was one cookie here or there? It wasn't nearly as big a deal as the promises she'd made to the most popular kids. She'd need to throw and attend various parties, as well as arrange for schoolwork to be done for some. And she'd help some to cheat on tests as well. Getting to the top took a lot of work.

"Oh, Dan"—Mom handed Dad his plate—"it's only a cookie. What's giving a few away going to hurt? Everyone does it. Don't you want your daughter to win?"

"Yeah, Daddy. Don't you want me to get into Yale?"

"This has nothing to do with college, Jennifer." He clacked his fork on the plate. "This has to do with doing the hard work of supporting her classmates and earning their respect. Not taking the easy way out."

Normally, Dad called Mom Jen. Now, the full name had come out. So not a good sign. This better not mean a fight was coming. Those were the worst. Time to smooth things over.

"Daddy, come on." She showed him her sad eyes. "Everybody makes campaign promises and gives gifts. I'm not the only one."

Of course, he didn't need to know she was the only person in the running who bribed the students with food and opportunities for cheating. Only two people had any hope of winning—herself and Harper Jones.

"People aren't objects to be used." Dad pushed his plate away, his eyes boring into hers. "You need to treat people with the respect they deserve, not provide empty promises you don't plan to honor."

"Daddy, I would never promise something I couldn't make good on." That wasn't exactly true. But close enough.

«»

The next evening, Lizzy and her mother spent hours perfecting the label for the cookie packages.

Vote Lizzy Tilbrook Class President—A friend you can count on!

The red border around the words gave it an extra touch of school spirit and matched the signs Ava plastered on the school walls that afternoon. Her friend had emailed her the calligraphy initials she'd designed for the posters so the labels would line up with the previous advertising.

The cookies would be a colossal hit with the students and

solidify the message. Vote for her, and sweet things would be on your plate in the future. It wasn't just a metaphor.

They were working at the kitchen island, well out of Dad's earshot. Mom would want to talk strategy once they were alone. Seriously, how had her parents, complete opposites, ever attracted each other in the first place, much less gotten married?

"Tell me more about Harper." Mom picked up a wrapped cookie. "What are her strengths and weaknesses? I need to know how to target her supporters. Maybe we can sway some of them in your direction."

"Ugh, Harper. She is such a Goody Two-shoes." Dangling her legs from the white metal barstool, Lizzy traced the marble along the waterfall countertop. Her lips pressed tight. How could she give a clear picture of her rival? "You know how Aunt Rebecca is always talking about helping the people who come to the mission?"

Just the name made her mother's eyes roll. "Who could forget? This month's newsletter showed her in full Mother Teresa mode. Even your cousin, Mary, had a photo op this time, teaching the kids in the school how to play guitar so they could all sing hymns together."

The newsletter always included a personal note from Dad's sister, and this month, Lizzy's cousin included a separate note addressed to her. Mom couldn't stand either of them.

Lizzy sneered. "Harper is at least as much a goody-goody as Mary."

Mom paused her hand movements as she stuck labels on cookie bags. "That bad, huh?"

"Worse." Lizzy leaned toward her. "Every morning, she tutors math students who are falling behind in their grades.

On summer break, she helps in the library, reading to the little kids."

Shaking her head, Mom pulled a label off the sheet, centered it on a cookie packet, and pressed it on to smooth the edges. "Do you think you could offer to tutor kids on a different subject? I know you said some of your classmates were struggling with science. You're good at that subject."

"Pfft. I'm good at every subject."

No need to be humble. Mom always said to play up your strengths when talking to those with influence. According to Mom, women needed to put themselves "out there" more. Let everyone know they weren't ashamed to be successful in a man's world. That was how Lizzy would get to the top.

"Of course, you are." Mom grinned back. "If you use your talents occasionally to help someone important, then you'll have another resource for the future. Did I ever tell you about how I helped the CEO out in my first job?"

Sigh. Not this story again.

"Yeah, you helped some lady who'd dropped her briefcase. The papers got caught in the wind, and you stopped to pick them up. Then you found out she was the new CEO. She helped you move up the ladder." Kicking her feet against the island, Lizzy pantomimed with her hands. "Blah, blah, blah. You've told me a million times."

Mom's lips twisted to the side, a sure sign she was thinking. "That was how I met Diane. She helped get me that first important promotion in the CPA firm. Of course, I'd have made partner even without her influence, but it's always nice to have someone important owe you a favor."

"You're at the top now, though." Lizzy stacked cookies into a rolling pack. "Now people need to kiss up to you."

"So true." A faraway look glazed Mom's eyes. "But I keep up my relationship at work with Diane. You never know what challenges life will bring or when you'll need to call on a resource."

She'd always thought of Diane as Mom's best friend. They never went out and did stuff together. No girls' spa days or even dinners at each other's homes. But they seemed friendly enough when they ran into each other in town or at the annual office picnic.

They finished applying the stickers to the treats within an hour.

One of the most important rules in Mom's playbook was to thank anyone who aided you.

People needed to see her as appreciative. If she made them feel good, they'd support her again.

"Thanks, Mom. I appreciate your help."

"You're welcome." Mom slid off her stool and stretched. Then her heels clacked on the hardwood floor as she walked away. "Good luck tomorrow."

«»

Lizzy pulled the cookie-filled rolling bag into the school the next morning. Ava waited beside her locker, as Lizzy instructed yesterday. Handing off the backpack, she provided guidance on the best way to use the treats to garner votes.

After verifying no teachers were around, Lizzy pinched her mask down to speak to Ava. "Make sure you remind people the cookie is from Lizzy as a 'friendly gesture.' It's important to emphasize my name and the word *friend*. Otherwise, it won't have as much impact. We want them to remember those two words together on Friday when they vote."

Ava straightened ramrod and tall, a soldier accepting a

mission, her dark bob a perfect helmet. "Got it. I won't let you down."

Biting her unmasked lower lip, Lizzy contemplated her buddy's serious demeanor. "Have fun with it, though. We don't want the students to think you're forced labor or something."

Ava's eyes widened and moved past Lizzy. Before Lizzy could turn, a hand landed on her left shoulder, an arm wrapped around her, and a warm body pressed against her right side.

Michael Flintwood's head was just inches above hers when she turned. She flipped her mask back in place and made sure her words came out adoringly. "Good morning, Michael. May we offer you a cookie?"

Ava's arm shoved a package into his mask. "It's a friendly gesture from Lizzy."

She cringed at the girl's enthusiasm. Ava stuck the cookie right up against Michael's nose as if she were trying to shove it up his nostrils. Lizzy reached out and nudged the proffered treat down.

"You know, 'vote for Lizzy.'" She chuckled, hoping Michael would see the humor in Ava's overdone fervor.

"Thanks." His eyes twinkled at Ava as he accepted the package. Then he saluted Lizzy with the cookie. "Tomorrow's the big day. You think you'll win? Harper has quite the following."

Her spine stiffened. "Pfft. Harper. She's a sweet kid and all, though she doesn't strike me as leader material. Does she?"

His only response was a shoulder shrug. Unwrapping the cookie, he pulled his mask down and bit into it. "Minnie's, huh?"

She grinned, forcing it to reach her eyes. "Only the best for my friends. Can I rely on your vote tomorrow?"

He looked down at the cookie, bit another chunk off, and

chewed. After he swallowed, he shifted his backpack to the opposite side of his body. "Yeah. I'll vote for you. You'll owe me a date for the next dance."

She sealed the deal with a playful punch to his arm. "Done."

«»

Today was the day. In a matter of time, Lizzy would accept the win. She'd been practicing her gracious acceptance and preparing to call her opponent a "good sport."

Voting happened during the students' lunch hour. Both candidates waited, eager for the results. By the time the last class rolled around, she had to have greeted every student in her class at least twice and promised dates, homework help, and party attendance—even a passing grade to a football player who struggled in his Earth and Space science class. She wasn't sure how she'd pull that one off. The guy was so disinterested in the subject, he could barely stay awake in class.

Whatever. A problem for another day.

As she sat in Algebra class, working math problems, the PA system sang to life with a musical tone. "Good afternoon," the principal said. "I know everyone is eager for the voting results."

This was it. Her big moment. She slid a mirror out of her book bag and checked her curls one last time. Not too much frizz.

The principal continued. "The sixth-grade class president this year will be Thomas Ferra. Congratulations, Thomas. The class vice president will be Connie Stroup."

Yes, that's nice. She didn't care about the sixth grade. *Move on already. What about the seventh grade?* Her race.

The principal's voice continued. "This year's seventh-grade class president will be Harper Jones. Congratulations, Harper. The class vice president will be Lizzy Tilbrook."

She froze. That couldn't be correct. He was going to correct his mistake. Wait for it. Harper couldn't have won.

Static crackled through the speaker. "And the eighth-grade…"

Nothing made sense. This wasn't the plan. She'd made all those promises. They'd eaten her cookies.

Confusion morphed into a slow burn. Raging heat flashed up the back of her neck. Her scalp itched. Fortunately, her mask hid the frown that mutated into a sneer.

How dare they vote Harper in instead of her?

Wait until Mom heard about this.

She'd know what to do.

After math, Lizzy didn't even wait for Ava after class. The last thing she needed was a rehash of the wretched campaign and what went wrong. She could picture her friend groveling and apologizing for mistakes that cost her the win. Normally, she loved to see Ava beg forgiveness, but she couldn't handle it right now.

The moment the end-of-day bell rang, she hustled to the girls' bathroom and waited for the hallway noises to subside before making her way to the school's front entrance. Just great. Dad's truck wasn't in the line of waiting parents. Late again, even on her big, not-so-big day. *Thanks, Dad.*

The buses had already exited the parking lot, so only a few students remained. At least Mom always insisted Lizzy didn't ride on the bus with the rest of the students.

Though Mom rarely made the trip to the school herself, she saved Lizzy from the rowdiness of public transportation. Mom had probably been the subject of torment in her early school days, but she'd never admitted it, just bragged about high school.

As Lizzy waited on a bench, she ground her teeth and jammed

her red Nikes against the cement sidewalk. Where had things gone wrong? And she'd made a ton of promises. Would her classmates expect her to keep all of them, even though she'd lost? She pressed a hand to the queasiness.

A honk brought her to her feet. Dad pulled up in his red Ford F-250 Super Duty. Her face flushed at the sight of his beat-up construction vehicle. Mom tried to convince him to trade it in for a new one, but he'd keep it until it died, claiming an early replacement would be a vanity purchase.

Once the truck came to a full stop, she scrambled into the cab and ripped her mask off. Hopefully, no one saw her get into the atrocity.

With ladders in its back, cement clumps on its bumper, and scratches and dents galore on its sides, she'd *die* if anyone important saw her today of all days. What was worse—her mother's pretentious status symbol or her father's complete rejection of status? Couldn't they just have normal vehicles?

"Good afternoon." Dad flashed a grin. "How was your day?"

No sense going into the election fiasco. He wouldn't understand. "Fine."

They drove away from the school, heading for home. "How'd the election go? Today was the big day, right?"

Shoot. No way to avoid the subject now. "I got the vice-president's role."

He patted her knee. "Congratulations! That's fantastic, sweetheart."

No reason to explain how *un*fantastic that was. He didn't get it. She needed to talk to Mom. Couldn't they just ride home in silence? Perhaps if she kept her mouth shut, he'd get the hint. She braced her elbow on her door and plunked her chin in her palm, facing the scenery whizzing by.

"What? No comment?" Dad never let a conversation die. "Aren't you excited?"

Frustration rose faster than she could tamp it down. Without thinking, she vomited her true thoughts. "No, Dad. I'm not excited. I can't believe that skank, Harper, beat me out for president, and I got stuck in second place."

Silence—she may have gone too far with the "skank" comment.

Well, maybe now that he knew how upset she was, he'd let it go.

"Skank, huh?"

Luck was not on her side today. She cringed at that soothing tone he used when he wanted to pacify Mom.

"That's a harsh term for Harper. From what I've heard, she's a nice gal. Did she do something wrong?"

Huffing, she crossed her arms over her chest. How could she make him understand? Harper was a skank just for existing. He'd never see what a pain it was going to be to honor all her campaign promises, knowing she'd lost anyway.

It wasn't just a single loss. It was a complete breakdown of her plan for Yale. She needed to be the class president throughout high school. That was the path to end up as president of the student body as a senior. She'd lost the first battle, perhaps the most important stepping-stone of the strategy.

"Dad, can we please just not talk about it? I need to talk to Mom. She understands."

He sucked in a deep breath through his nose and slowly released it through his mouth. His calming technique. Another trick he used when he got into fights with Mom.

Great. Now he was angry. Best to make nice right away. She didn't need him all riled up when they got home.

She sighed. "Sorry, Dad. Harper's not a skank. Not really. I'm just upset."

He reached over and patted her knee once more. It might as well have been her head, as if she were a dog that had performed well—because a performance was exactly what it was. Only Mom would understand Harper truly was a skank.

«»

Later that evening, Lizzy scowled while Dad explained the situation to Mom as she entered the dining room for dinner. Having him break the news was better. She couldn't have done it without calling Harper names again. Mom avoided eye contact during the quiet meal.

After dinner, Mom tidied up the kitchen while Dad sat in the living room, taking in the evening news. This was the perfect time to connect with Mom without Dad's interference.

Lizzy slipped into the kitchen, ready for some girl time. "So... you know about the election."

Mom turned the water off in the island sink, wiped her hands on a towel, and looked Lizzy square in the face. "What's your plan?"

That stumped her. Lizzy edged up to the island across from her. "M–my plan?"

With her hands braced on either side of her, Mom leaned against the marble and narrowed her focus on Lizzy. "Are you going to let Harper take over without fighting back?"

Her temples throbbed. What was she missing?

"The election is over. What can I do now?"

A slow smile curved Mom's face until it twisted into a smirk. "You know what they say. All's fair in love and war. You may have lost one battle to Harper, but you can still win the war."

War? What war? Was Mom losing it?

Arms folded across her chest, Lizzy waited.

"Look." Mom came around the island and hushed her tones with a glance toward the living room. "Just because Harper is the president now doesn't mean she will be all year. Sometimes people get kicked out of their positions. I can't tell you how many times I've seen it in the corporate world."

Just what did business life have to do with school? "Why would Harper get kicked out of the president's role?"

"Because she'll get caught copying from someone else on a test or stealing the teacher's answer sheet or something even worse."

Now Lizzy narrowed her own eyes at her mother. "I don't think that'll happen. She's a perfect student. She'd never do any of that stuff."

"Maybe not on her own." Mom winked. "But with a little help, who knows what she might get caught at? Are you tracking?"

Oh yes. She was tracking, all right. Yes, indeed.

«»

Lizzy didn't want to get out of bed on Monday. The thought of school nauseated her. How could she face all the students who voted for Harper instead of her? She had no way of even knowing who'd supported her.

No way would she honor all those promises she'd made. People couldn't expect her to after she'd lost. After all, how could she know who'd honored their deals and who hadn't?

She flopped onto her side, scowling at the checkerboard tile floor, the room with its white walls, drapes, and fluffy white rug and bedding accented by her hard black enamel desk, headboard, and nightstand. The opposing furniture and décor poised like chess pieces set to remind her life was a game you played to win. Was Mom right? Was there a way to steal the president's role from her opponent? They'd talked about options for an hour before Dad interrupted their discussion the previous evening.

Dad was a lot like Aunt Rebecca. He was always the glass-half-full version of Mom's half-empty attitude. Hot and cold. Proof opposites attracted.

Huffing, Lizzy scrambled out of bed. Hands fisting, she kicked her beanbag chair as she passed, the slouchy purple the only brightness in her room, her only expression of her true self. That and her bright clothes. She picked those clothes carefully for the battle of the day, then hefted her book bag onto one shoulder, and headed through the game room and down the hall. Whispered argument emanated from the kitchen. She approached without announcing herself and paused outside the room, out of sight.

Dad spoke. "You two were plotting something last night."

"You don't need to be involved in every conversation between Lizzy and me." The words seethed from Mom. "Some things a mother and daughter need to work out on their own."

"That didn't sound like mother-daughter bonding time. You're hiding something. You both are. I know how your mind works, Jennifer. Don't lead your daughter down the wrong path."

"Me?" Her voice shrilled higher, not yelling, but losing control. "Look at the example you've set. You could have been the CEO of your own construction company by now if you'd put effort into it."

"I'm not interested in having my own company." Yep, that placating tone again. "I like what I do. I enjoy being one of the guys. Climbing the corporate ladder has always been your thing, not mine. Let's not change the subject, though. This isn't about our jobs. It's about our daughter and what we're teaching her."

That proved Lizzy didn't want them to continue. When they reached this point, it always went downhill. Time to end it.

She popped through the doorway and forced a smile. "Good morning. Who's dropping me off at school today?"

Both her parents turned to her with fake grins.

Dad spoke first. "Morning, sweetie. Did you sleep well?"

He smothered her in a hug before she could pass by, always the parent who showed physical affection. She returned the embrace. "I slept fine, thanks."

Mom moved to zip her laptop bag, then handed her an envelope. "It's a letter from your cousin. I found it in the mail Saturday, along with Aunt Rebecca's monthly newsletter from the orphanage."

Lizzy accepted the envelope and slid it into her book bag. "I'll read it later. So, who's on school drop-off duty?"

"That would be me," Mom said. "Your father has to be on the jobsite early this morning."

With that quick nonverbal exchange between her parents, if Lizzy were a betting person, she'd have wagered Mom decided moments ago. Dad couldn't argue without causing a scene, and he didn't like to fight in front of her—a fact Mom took advantage of often.

Seriously, did her parents think they were hiding all this from her? Her courses weren't the only thing she studied—Mom herself taught the importance of studying people.

Time to end the tension. Lizzy headed for the door. "Let's go then."

On their way toward the school, Mom broke the silence. "Keep your eye out for an opportunity today. You've got the ideas we came up with last night, right?"

Lizzy rolled her eyes. They'd discussed several ways to get Harper into trouble at school. She wasn't sure she could pull any of them off, but she'd keep watch for the chance. "I've got it. Okay?"

"No need to get huffy with me, young lady. I'm just trying to help."

She didn't respond, and they rode the rest of the way in silence.

They pulled up to the pharmacy down the block from the school. She opened her door to escape the confines of the vehicle.

"Have a good day," her mother chimed as Lizzy stepped onto the sidewalk.

She wiggled the dreaded mask out of her tight jeans pocket and looped it onto her ears before responding. "Yes, ma'am. You too."

Once inside the school, she made her way to the desk where Ava awaited.

Her friend fidgeted, a familiar twitch in her left eye as if she dreaded meeting up.

"Hey, Ava." Lizzy took her seat.

"You okay? I didn't see you after school Friday."

She couldn't avoid the botched election forever. Best to get the discussion out of the way. "I'm good. It's fine. Really."

With her eyes narrowing like that, Ava wasn't convinced. "I got here early today and took all the posters down."

Wasn't that just like her friend to think ahead and step up before Lizzy even thought to ask? Too bad it came across as groveling. Maybe she needed a BFF with a stronger personality.

Perhaps that would be the key to winning next time.

For now, though, she needed to maintain the resources she had. Letting the fake smile return to her eyes, she reached out and squeezed her so-called BFF's hands. "Thanks, Ava. You're a good friend."

Ava's tentative grin, though hidden behind her mask, crinkled up her eyes and spoke volumes.

"Michael was looking for you this morning."

The opening bell rang, and the overhead speaker crackled to life, saving Lizzy from any further conversation.

As the morning announcements droned on, she slid her cousin's letter out of her book bag and opened it.

Lizzy,

I hope this letter finds you doing well. The current variant wave is disrupting the mission. We aren't certain we'll be able to stay open much longer. Mom's worried about me living here now. She's even threatened to send me back to the States.

I can't imagine leaving her here alone to run everything. It seems like I'd be abandoning her in her moment of need.

Please say a prayer for us and the people we serve here as I continue to pray for you, Uncle Daniel, and Aunt Jennifer.

Write soon. I always love to hear how you're doing in school.

Love,

Mary

A shudder coursed through her. What would it be like to live in a poor country, giving up the everyday conveniences of the modern world? In some letters, Mary talked about students coming to school just to get food.

Dad thought Lizzy should spend the summer before her senior year serving at the mission. He'd said it would help her appreciate the blessings of living in a wealthy country.

No way. Let her aunt and cousin do mission work if they

enjoyed it. She would enjoy her cheeseburgers and American Eagle clothing, thank you very much.

Besides, there were more important operations here. She had an election to win back. Her focus should be there. How could she discredit Harper?

3

Chapter Three

The television was on when Lizzy came through the great room Thursday, ready for school. Strange. Her parents hardly ever watched the morning news shows. Something had to be going on. She headed to the study.

Dad stood in front of the enormous flat screen as images of Honduras flashed across it. At the sight of Lizzy, he pulled her to his side, squeezing her tight. "Your aunt Rebecca called this morning." His voice cracked. "She's sending Mary here before they close the borders. We're afraid it will happen soon."

The camera panned images of bodies lined up next to hospitals and rural health centers. Workers had only covered the heads. The reporter indicated they'd depleted their stock of body bags. Corpses burning in pyres flashed across the screen. Knowing her aunt and cousin were there sent a chill up her spine. These weren't nameless faces. Dad knew people in the area from the mission trips he'd been on.

A tear escaped his eye and slide down his cheek. He didn't bother to wipe it away, and she couldn't look any longer. "When will Mary arrive?"

Dad cleared his throat with a wet cough. His words came out soggy. "I'll pick her up at the airport today if she passes both variant tests. She has to test negative before getting on the plane, and then again before she can pass through customs."

While Lizzy didn't relish having her cousin living with them, seeing her father hurting this way was hard. It would be a tremendous blow to him if something happened to either Aunt Rebecca or Mary.

He whispered with his eyes closed, praying indecipherable, almost silent words. Tears pooled in her eyes.

Heels clacking in the kitchen alerted her to Mom's presence. With a quick squeeze, Lizzy released herself from his grip, swiped at her eyes, and joined her mother.

Dad needed space to compose himself. If Mom knew he was in the other room praying, she'd say something derogatory. Faith was a heated subject in their family at the best of times. She'd seen pictures of her parents as teenagers at church youth-group events. Now, she couldn't imagine her mother as a church member. What happened to move Mom away from faith while Dad clung to portions of it?

Prayer to a god was an uneducated worldview. Still, Lizzy couldn't help but feel her father's pain at the death surrounding the people he knew and loved in Honduras.

She'd do her best to run interference until he composed himself. Starting the day with them in a fight was never fun. "Dad said Aunt Rebecca is sending Mary to stay with us. Were you planning on giving her the guest room? I can put the linens in the wash if you'd like."

"Already done. Thank you, though."

Of course, Mom would be on top of things. The news report stopped. Dad had clicked off the television. Lizzy just needed to give him a few more minutes to get himself sorted out.

"Would you like me to stop in the school office to see what we need to do to get Mary enrolled?"

Mom's eyes widened. "I hadn't even thought of that. You're right, though. It could be months before she can go home. If you could find out what paperwork is involved or whatever, I can follow up with the principal."

While Lizzy didn't want to do the legwork to get her cousin enrolled, she'd keep the peace any way she could. When Dad walked into the kitchen, his eyes looked a bit red but dry. Mom wouldn't even notice.

Now a bit more distraction should ease him into the conversation. "I'm going to stop by the office today to see about registering Mary."

He smiled and rubbed her shoulder. "Good idea. Thank you, sweetie. Your cousin will need a friend to help her through the transition. She'll be stressed out by the time she gets here. It will be good for her to have you to hang out with."

Nuts. That hadn't occurred to her.

How embarrassing! She'd have to drag her cousin around to all the classrooms, make introductions, and show her the ropes. Mary wasn't exactly a fashionista. They definitely didn't have name-brand clothing at the mission. All her cousin's pictures showed her in dowdy dresses and long skirts. Like a nun.

No way could she let her cousin ruin her rep. Mary would have to change her style to hang out with her. Imagining her cousin dressed in designer jeans brought a chuckle to her lips.

"What's so funny?" Mom stared at her with the hint of a smile, ready to be let in on the joke.

If it were only Mom in the room, Lizzy would've shared her thoughts. Dad eyed her intently, though, and a joke at his niece's expense wouldn't help right now.

"Nothing. Just thinking of taking Mary shopping when she gets here. She won't be able to pack enough for a full-time move to the States."

"That's so sweet of you." He pulled his wallet out of his pocket, opened it, and removed five twenty-dollar bills, then handed them to Lizzy. "Let me know if you need any more."

She looked at the crisp bills, then at her mother. The last thing she wanted to do right now was upset her father. What he'd given her might cover one pair of the right jeans, but that was all. Did he expect her to take Mary shopping at the thrift store or something?

Mom rolled her eyes. "I doubt a hundred dollars is going to cut it, Dan." She patted Lizzy's shoulder. "We'll all go together. Girls' day out."

Whew! Lizzy let out a held breath. Mom would know what to do. She stole a glance at her father, and he shrugged. Good. He wasn't upset.

Her frumpy cousin would probably land Lizzy a few new outfits. This might end up being an excellent opportunity.

Mom kept her to a strict clothing budget each month. Not nearly enough to keep ahead of some of her peers, but she did the best she could. She had an image to maintain.

Though Dad would never understand, Mom did.

«»

At school, Lizzy headed for the administration office. She walked through the door where Mrs. Burns sat tall and regal behind the counter at a desk covered in cat paraphernalia. Everyone called her the cat lady behind her back. They often made meowing or purring sounds when they saw her in the hallways.

Pictures of at least eight distinct animals cluttered her desk and the wall behind it. One frame, about twice the size of the others, contained a photo of herself with a man who had to be her husband. Included in the photo were four cats. They each held one in their arms, one sat on his shoulder, and one had wrapped itself around her neck. The cat necklace, combined with Mrs. Burns's curly dark hair, made her look as though she were wearing a fur in some throwback to the sixties.

The secretary looked up from the computer and addressed Lizzy as she shut the door. "How may I help you today?"

Mrs. Burns's face mask was a yawning cat's mouth. The sight distracted Lizzy until she almost forgot why she was there. How could anyone wear something so hideous?

"Dear?"

That single word brought her out of her inner thoughts. "I'm looking for instructions on how to register my cousin at school here. She'll be living with us for a while, but we're not sure how long."

The cat's mouth moved on Mrs. Burns's face as her eyebrows rose in question. "Is she from the local area?"

She needed to stop focusing on the mask, or she'd never get to class on time. "My aunt is a missionary in Honduras. The variant is getting bad there right now, so my cousin is moving to the States for a while. Is there a form or something for us to fill out?"

At the mention of a form, Mrs. Burns sprang into action, fingers flying over the keyboard with rapid tappity-taps. A printer behind her hummed to life, and three sheets of paper spit out the top. She picked the papers up and walked them over to Lizzy, placing the set on the counter separating them.

"She'll need to provide some sort of identification with proof of age. Hopefully, they have an ID in Honduras. I don't know much about that country. Fill out the forms and have them notarized. Include proof of residency. Acceptable forms of verification are on the last page here."

With a pen that must work double duty as a cat toy, she circled a section on the sheet. The strokes of the ballpoint caused a feather, tied with a long string to the top, to swirl around the desk. If one of Mrs. Burns's cats was on the counter, Lizzy could imagine it chasing the plume. Her eyes followed the movement.

Focus, Lizzy. Stay on task. "Besides the form, the ID, and the proof of residency, what else will we need?"

In her matter-of-fact voice, Mrs. Burns pointed to another section and drew a star next to a line. "The last item will be proof of current vaccination status. Not the variant, mind you, but the usual: Tdap, flu, chickenpox, MMR, and hepatitis B. It's all there."

Lizzy's eyes watered, and her throat itched. Cat hair coated Mrs. Burns's sweater sleeves. Great. Even though the cat wasn't with her, she'd brought the allergen along for the ride. Time to scoot. If Mom had questions, she could call.

"Thank you. We'll get all this back to you soon."

She didn't wait to stuff the papers into her backpack before jetting out the door, back to the fresh air in the hallway. A quick peek at her watch spurred her into a jog.

«»

The teacher handed out study sheets in science class later in the day—at least twenty pages of outline for the first half of their textbook.

A groan came from someone two desks ahead of her. Harper flipped through the notes. Although the new class president tutored others in math and read to preschoolers, Harper hated science, her worst subject.

That sparked an idea. This was her chance. Harper had to maintain a B average to keep her status as class president. The pressure would be on.

Lizzy scribbled a quick note.

Want to study together? I can help you ace this test. Text me. 555-436-2986. Lizzy.

A tap on the shoulder of the girl in front of her and a whispered request was all it took for the note to make its way up the row to Harper.

As soon as she read the note, Harper faced Lizzy with a quick nod. A grateful smile crinkled up her green eyes.

Bull's-eye.

The plan hadn't fully formed in Lizzy's head yet, but if she could pull her rival into a closer "friendship," the sabotage opportunities would grow exponentially.

The tricky part would be discrediting Harper without implicating herself in the downfall. It wouldn't do for their classmates to see Lizzy target her rival. Best to look quite the opposite.

After the class-ending bell sounded, Harper waited for her by the door. She twisted a lock of brunette hair around a finger, the nervous fidget revealing her opponent was uncomfortable. She pulled down her mask and spoke in low tones, not quite a whisper. "Thank you for offering to help me out. I don't know why I struggle so much in this class. It's the only one."

Too bad Lizzy couldn't take that anxiety and rub it in for good measure, but that wouldn't endear her to Harper. Instead, after verifying no teacher was looking, Lizzy nudged her own mask down. "It's okay. We all have a subject we're weaker in than others. Not sure which mine is, but I'm sure someday a class will be hard for me."

Harper wrinkled her forehead, blinking rapidly. "Really? You don't struggle with any classes? That's amazing."

This was Lizzy's opportunity to shine. "Dad says I'm a natural at schoolwork."

What her father actually said was that God had blessed her with a gifted mind that could absorb information in the classroom. But Harper didn't need to hear about blessings and gifts. This wasn't a Catholic school run by nuns, after all.

The other girl shrugged off the comment. "So, when did you want to get together? You are welcome to come over to my place after school anytime. Or I can come to yours?"

Mom might as well meet Harper and get a good sense of what they were up against. "Let's study at my place, if you don't mind. Text me, and I'll send you my address. Can someone pick you up at our place if you ride home with me later this week?"

Harper dug her cell out of her backpack. "I'll text my mom and make sure it's okay. I'll let you know before the end of the day. Sound good?"

Lizzy nodded, and they went their separate ways. It sounded good, all right. Very good. This was going to be fun.

4

Chapter Four

When Lizzy stepped out of Mom's car, Dad's truck was already in the garage. He'd made it home from the airport in record-breaking time. Atlanta traffic could be brutal during the day, and the snarl of airport traffic added to the fun and games. But this latest strain of the variant had people working from home again, freeing up the highways.

Lizzy sucked in a deep breath before following her mother into the house. Though her cousin was as backwater as they came, Lizzy still felt inferior to Mary in some respects. And Mary's friendly aura made Lizzy uncomfortable.

It was as if Mary knew some secret about the world Lizzy just couldn't figure out. Her cousin seemed so serene and at peace, even when something bad was going on. It was just too weird. Though Lizzy would love to have the same feeling she imagined Mary had, she didn't understand where it came from or how her cousin held onto it.

"We're home." Mom sailed through the door into the mudroom and then on to the kitchen, her pumps clacking on the hardwood. "Where's our guest hanging out?"

Lizzy followed her mother through to where Dad sat at the kitchen island. He drank from a glass of water. Mary pivoted on the stool next to him and offered a shy wave. Her head at that angle put the Tilbrook nose into focus. It looked good on Dad, strong, but Mom always said Lizzy was lucky not to get it. Somehow, though, it added interest to Mary's face and made her unique.

Lizzy scrunched her generic little nose up. Would wearing a mask would feel different with the Tilbrook nose?

"Welcome home. Mary and I just got here." He gave Mom a peck on the cheek as she breezed by, ignoring his attempted hug. "We were hydrating after Mary's long day of travel."

"How are you, dear?" Mom parked her rolling bag next to the refrigerator. "You must be exhausted. Was your flight smooth at least?"

Mary's smile was genuine, though her eyes blinked a few times as if she wanted to close them for a nap and the off-kilter bun atop her head had slipped to the left. "It was fine, thank you. The longest part of the trip was getting from the mission to the airport in Honduras. It's a seven-hour drive from El Mirador."

"You poor thing." Mom soothed, but Lizzy knew better. "Lizzy, take your cousin and show her where she'll be staying."

Dad stood. "I'll get her bags. There isn't much. She travels light." He smiled at his niece as he headed toward the garage.

"Come on," Lizzy said. "Your room is right next to mine."

Mary hopped off her stool, carried her empty glass to the sink, then followed Lizzy.

They went through the dining room and the game room. Then Lizzy pointed to the door on their right. "You're in here."

She opened the door and led her cousin into the spacious

bedroom. After she flipped the lights on, she continued into the attached bathroom, turning on the lights over the sink and in the adjacent closet.

"I've got my own bathroom?" Mary's eyes grew wide as she wandered into the room and stared at the recessed tub. She opened the linen closet, then peeked into the large walk-in closet. "I can't imagine needing this enormous closet to myself. I'm not taking your room, am I? Where do you sleep?"

Her cousin's open mouth would capture flies if she didn't get it under control soon. *Get a grip, girl. Surely, you've seen a modern house before.*

"I'm just across the hallway, and I've got my bathroom and closet, so this is all yours." Crossing her arms over her chest, Lizzy cocked a hip against the doorway. "How long has it been since you've visited the States, anyway?"

Mary eyed the ceiling and tapped her fingers against her chin a few times as if counting in her head. "I guess it's been two years. We don't come to the States often, and when we do, we're touring the various churches. Mom does a slide show of the mission and the projects we're working on. If it wasn't for fundraising, we wouldn't come up much at all. There's too much to do at the mission."

When she shrugged, her matter-of-fact look implied Lizzy should know what it was like to live on a mission in a third-world country. But everything she knew came from reading the letters her cousin and aunt sent.

One look at Mary's current attire assured Lizzy she wanted nothing to do with missionary life. Mary had twisted her long sandy brown hair in a tight bun atop her head with no blingy band, no styling, no makeup. Her generic jeans had no rhinestones, no fancy threading, nothing to make them stand out. Her T-shirt must have been a donation from the States back in the eighties if the soda advertisement on it gave any indication.

Dad came through the open bedroom door with a large duffle and a backpack. "Bags on the bed?"

"Thank you, yes."

At Mary's grateful smile, Lizzy stifled a guilty cringe.

The bags thudded onto the plush sage-gray comforter. Mom's color choice was supposed to be soothing and keep guests compliant—not that they had company often.

"Need anything else before I watch the news?" Dad asked.

Mary moved toward the bed and unzipped her duffle bag. "No thank you, Uncle Dan."

"I'll let you get situated before supper." Lizzy backed toward the doorway. "I left shampoo and such in the bathroom. Let me know if you need anything else."

Ugh. The sweet smile was back out on display.

"That was kind of you. I'm sure I'll be fine."

During dinner, Mom shared the plan for a shopping trip.

"Oh, we don't need to do that." Mary shook her head so hard her bun slipped a little further left. "I've got plenty to wear. It's a little wrinkled from the trip, but I can just fluff it in the dryer."

"Nonsense." Mom waved a hand. "Every girl needs a few new outfits when they start at a new school."

Mary's face blotched with red spots. "I didn't bring much money with me."

Dad jumped into the conversation before Mom's opening mouth could utter her next words. "We've got it, Mary. Don't worry about the money. We owe you a few birthday presents." He winked at his niece.

The next morning, Lizzy arrived in the kitchen eager for

shopping and found Mary dressed and ready to go. Her clothes were wrinkle-free and tidy, but not this year's Forever 21 styles. The silky ponytail she sported, so different from the frizzy one Lizzy often fought with, was perfect, though, and she pulled off the hobo look with a cute short-sleeved blouse, clean jeans, and the same pair of Nikes from yesterday. Her battered backpack waited on the white barstool beside her, and with her elbows braced on the marble island, she held a mug between two hands, balanced above a slice of peanut butter toast on her plate.

She beamed at Lizzy. "Good morning, coz."

Nuts. Her cousin was a morning person. Lizzy suppressed the groan that ached to escape. This was one of those mornings she wished she drank coffee. The scent from the coffee maker was enough to make her want to try the horrid brew again.

"Mom said we'd stop at the school after the mall and drop off the paperwork to get you registered." She fished a packet of hot cocoa from the pantry and placed a mug of water in the microwave. "Hopefully, you'll start school on Monday."

Mary took a generous sip from her mug and swallowed. "I can't believe your mom is letting you skip school on a Friday to go shopping."

"I don't need to go to school every day. It's straightforward stuff for me, and I can get A's without having to sit through every class." The microwave dinged, and she removed the mug and poured the cocoa mix in. "You looking forward to going to school in the States? Must be a lot different from the mission."

Mary tilted her head to the side and shrugged. "Not sure, honestly. I know it'll be different. Mom said girls can be cruel here sometimes. We all work together on school assignments at the mission. You can learn a lot more when you help others to understand the concepts."

That reminded Lizzy of the Earth and Space science exam coming up. She needed to get Harper over for a tutoring lesson. But that was a problem for tomorrow. Today was all about shopping.

Mom rushed into the kitchen and headed for the coffeepot and the mug tree. "You two ready to go? Lots to get done today, and I need to be sure I'm back in time for an online conference call later this afternoon."

Double nuts. When Mom had a timetable to keep, shopping would be more a mission than an experience. Say goodbye to a sit-down lunch at a restaurant. It would be a drive-thru for sure. "We're just waiting for you."

«»

On the home stretch of the mall crawl, they'd hit every store worth shopping on the trek from the parking entrance to the building's far end and were halfway back on the return trip. The weight of the packages now slowed their progression.

"No Bath and Body Works stop today, please?" Lizzy whined. Still, her mother's favorite store would be their next detour. "I don't think my arms will hold out much longer."

Though their trip's purpose had been to refresh Mary's wardrobe, Lizzy's had expanded significantly. Who could pass up a sale, especially when they were swiping her mother's credit card and not Lizzy's debit card?

Mom's power walk paused. Her mother's face was hard to decipher, with blank eyes, as if Lizzy'd interrupted her mental wanderings. "Do you think you have enough for your first week, Mary? We could always shop again next weekend, but I'm booked until then."

Mary, who'd trailed behind, puffed at the hair that had freed itself from her ponytail and flopped into her eyes. "I can't imagine I'll need to shop again for a year. We shouldn't have spent this much on clothes. Like I said, I've got plenty already."

There she went again, insisting she didn't need much. Lizzy's count of packages revealed more hanging on her arms than her cousin's. It had been a good day. "Let's knock off now. We could stop at Minnie's for a bite before we drop the paperwork off at the school."

Why not make a play for proper food instead of a drive-thru burger? Mom wouldn't be able to resist the idea of being able to grab supper. Efficiency was key to her.

A smile brightened Mom's face. "Perfect. We'll pick up dinner at the same time."

Bull's-eye!

A quick sit-down lunch with carryout for supper got them to the school just before the end-of-day bell rang. They waited in the car while Mom ran to turn in the registration paperwork.

"Do you like your school?" Mary asked. "Have a lot of friends?"

Lizzy twisted in the front passenger seat to see her cousin. Crammed in the two-door Lexus's back, Mary retied her loose ponytail while staring at the building. She'd look so good with a sparkling nose stud.

Hmm. How to define a friend? Ava was always around, of course, and probably thought she was Lizzy's BFF. She'd never dissuaded her from the idea, but did that make them besties?

She shared with others only in limited spurts, but not a soul in that building knew her inner thoughts. Mom always said letting others in too deep made you weak—gave others too much control over you. But how to explain that to Mary? "I'll introduce you to Ava on Monday. She's the one I hang out with the most. But as the class vice president, I know almost everyone in my class."

That drew her cousin's attention from the building. Her hazel eyes widened to the size of quarters. "Class vice president? I didn't realize you were so popular and well connected. That's wonderful. I worried I wouldn't be able to make friends."

The way Mary relaxed back against the seat set Lizzy on edge.

Huh. Her cousin didn't understand how this worked. She'd lost the election to Harper. Letting the conversation die a natural death was easier than explaining the intricacies of the election process.

The driver's door opened, and Mom slid back in. "You're all set, Mary. Just need to stop in the office on Monday morning and pick up your schedule. They're going to mirror Lizzy's, so you'll have an extra boost of help to acclimate you to the classwork."

"Thank you so much." Mary's smile twinkled, and then she scooted forward and threw her arms around Lizzy from the back. "We're going to be classmates. I can't wait to meet all your friends."

The hug threw her. It was like being held captive in a vise. She barely knew her cousin from the letters she'd received over the years, and now Mary acted as if they were besties. Lizzy tentatively patted Mary's back. "Yes. Monday should be interesting."

Very interesting, indeed.

5

Chapter Five

Lizzy felt like a long-tailed cat in a room full of rocking chairs as she walked out of the school administrative offices. It wasn't the best way to start a Monday morning. Mrs. Burns rambled for at least fifteen minutes about the process she'd gone through to ensure Mary would be in every class Lizzy was in. Wasn't that just lovely?

Somehow, it didn't feel spectacular. Mary's lips had to hurt with that huge smile pushing her cheeks up above her mask. She'd chattered about school all morning, so Lizzy started mentally filtering the babble out.

They made it to homeroom just before the late bell and scurried to the back desks where Ava waited with narrowed eyes. Ava mouthed the silent words. *Who's that?*

As the overhead speaker buzzed to life, the principal started the morning announcements. Lizzy moved toward her seat and pointed to an empty spot for Mary. Before taking the desk in front of her friend, she leaned into Ava's ear and whispered. "My cousin from Honduras. She's staying with us for a while."

Ava nodded and gave Mary a small wave. As soon as they

moved to the hallway to transition to their next classroom, Ava claimed the spot between Lizzy and Mary for their walk, her attention on Mary. "Morning. I'm Lizzy's BFF, Ava. And you're Lizzy's cousin?"

"I'm Mary, and it's such a pleasure meeting Lizzy's best friend." Mary hooked her arm through Ava's as if they'd been friends forever and just met up again in the school hallway. "We're going to see a lot of each other. I'll do my best not to get in the way, though. I'm sure the class vice president has a lot of work to do."

Ava leaned into Mary with a stage whisper. "Oh, she's busy all right. We hardly ever get together outside of school. She's always unavailable. I've got plenty of free time, though."

Groan. Lizzy could just picture the two of them heading off to a party without her. "I'm right here, ladies. You act as if I'm off on the moon somewhere."

The two giggled—yes, actually giggled—like they were back in elementary school. The edges of her mouth flattened out. Sometimes the mask could be a blessing.

Mary released Ava's arm and pulled out her schedule. "Are you in all of Lizzy's classes with her? Mrs. Burns was so sweet and fit me in to match Lizzy's schedule."

Ava squealed. "That's fantastic! All three of us will be together the whole day. We'll be like the Three Musketeers."

Lizzy rolled her eyes. They'd be suggesting matching T-shirts before she knew it. How could these two be instant friends? And just who was she more embarrassed by, Ava or Mary?

"Speaking of class, we'd better get moving, or we're going to be late for science."

They arrived at the room, and Ava guided Mary to a nearby available desk. When she crossed toward her seat, Harper caught Lizzy's attention, stopping her as she passed by.

"Is tonight good for you to study?" Harper tapped a pencil's eraser side on her desktop. "We don't have much time left. The test is Friday."

Mary's arrival messed up Lizzy's routine. She'd even forgotten about Harper and the test.

Watching her cousin greeting everyone as if they'd been friends forever, Lizzy wavered in her resolve to carry out the plan.

It was a solid plan, but devious. What would it be like to have friends like Mary was making, instead of resources, like her relationship with Ava? If she followed through with the scheme, there would be no taking it back.

"Why don't you come over after school on Thursday?" The resolve to follow through struck home, and she smiled at her adversary. "We'll have you sporting an *A* in no time."

Harper's return grin was a reward in itself. "Can I ride with you? I'll text my mom to pick me up after?"

"Perfect." Yes, indeed. It was perfect. Once again—bull's-eye.

«»

The three of them sat in Lizzy's room. Harper rested at the small but functional black enamel desk, Lizzy sat cross-legged on the bed, and Mary splayed in the giant purple beanbag chair.

"Ugh, I'll never remember all of this." Harper slapped her book closed. "What's that mnemonic again?"

"This isn't rocket science. It's earth and space science—much easier." Lizzy rolled her eyes. "My Very Excellent Mom Just Served Us Noodles."

"Who talks like that anyway?" Harper's griping amped up with her frustration. "Mars, Venus, Earth, Mom... Mom..."

"You started with Mars. It's supposed to be Mercury. Remember? That's probably why you can't remember the second *M*." Mary scooted off the beanbag and shook her arms. Then she lay on the floor, planted her feet, and arched her back to form a letter M with her legs. "The first *M* is the tiny planet—close to the sun—hot stuff. Remember?"

"Mercury." Harper groaned. "Venus, Earth, Mars, Jupiter, Saturn—Uranus, Neptune."

"Yay!" Mary popped into a stand and shook imaginary pom-poms. "Go Harper, go Harper, go!"

Lizzy laughed as her cousin's gyrations became more dramatic and her body formed each of the letters of the mnemonic.

"M, My, Mercury—" Mary chanted, and Harper repeated. Harper jumped in with the cheer beside Mary. "V, Very, Venus—"

Lizzy wanted in on the activity after hours of dull study. She scurried off the bed and created the next letter with her arms. "E, Excellent, Earth."

Each letter of the phrase came out louder than the last until by the end they were shouting the words.

"N, Noodles, Neptune!" all three shrieked the last word, jumped around waving their arms, and screamed as if they'd just won the state championship.

A banging on the door captured their attention. Dad bellowed from the other side. "Harper, your mom's here."

"Coming!" Lizzy hollered back. The trio dissolved into giggles as they dropped onto the bed.

After they'd caught their breath, Harper groaned and sprang to her feet. As she stuffed her text into her book bag, she smiled. "I'd better get out there. Better get some shut-eye in before the big test. Right?"

"You're going to do great." Mary danced over to Harper and

threw her arms around the other girl. "I just know it."

Harper returned Mary's hug while Lizzy stood near the door, stuck in an invisible force field.

She'd never hugged a friend before. And here, Mary spent only a few hours studying with Harper, and she just threw her arms around her. As if it were the most normal thing in the world to do.

What would it take to have friends like that? She'd never hugged Ava.

Come to think of it, she rarely embraced her mother either. Mom didn't often show physical affection, but Dad did. She'd always been Daddy's Princess, and he'd wrapped his arms around her at the slightest whim. Mom always gave a perfunctory squeeze, but it never felt as warm and welcoming as Dad's cozy snuggles.

Harper and Mary released each other before they strode over to the door Lizzy'd opened. Before she could even react, Harper threw her arms around her.

"Thank you so much." Harper's whisper was warm in her ear. "I don't know what I would have done without you two."

Mechanically, Lizzy brought her hands up to pat Harper on the back. "No problem. What are friends for?"

The embrace felt wrong. She felt like such a traitor, her plan weighing on her.

Now could she follow through? Maybe they were friends after all.

They trooped out of the bedroom, through the game room and dining room, and into the kitchen.

Harper's mom sat on one of the kitchen island barstools but stood as the girls entered.

"How'd the study session go?" Harper's mom asked. "Ready

for the big test?"

Harper shrugged. "Well…"

"She's going to do great." Mary jumped in, throwing her arm around the other girl's shoulder.

Harper grinned back and nodded.

"Excellent. Let's head for home and get you rested up." Harper's mom turned to Lizzy's mom. "Thank you again for having Harper over. This study session meant a lot to her. She was so afraid of getting a poor grade on the test."

Mom winked. "You know how these overachievers get. Right?"

"That I do." Harper's mom winked back.

Mom's lips twitched up in a smile. Lizzy could see the fake behind it, but no one else seemed any the wiser. "Anytime, my dear. We're happy to have her."

Lizzy hadn't realized she was holding her breath until Mom closed the door behind their company. She wasn't sure why she'd been holding it, though. What did she think Mom would do, yell at their guests? That wasn't how Mom worked. When Mom struck, it would mimic a hidden cobra, not a charging bull.

"I'm exhausted." Mary yawned and stretched for the ceiling. "Time to hit the hay myself. That study session got me ready for the test tomorrow too. But this princess needs her rest."

"Good night, dear," Mom said to Mary while she put a firm hand on Lizzy's arm. "Have a good sleep."

Mom wanted her to stay while Mary danced off to her bedroom.

As soon as the two of them were alone in the kitchen, the fake smile vanished. "You ready for the test?"

"Yes, I'm good."

"Have everything readied to go?"

"I got it already. You don't need to keep reminding me. I'm not a child."

"Just making sure. No need to get all bent out of shape."

"Pfft." Lizzy blew air out and rolled her eyes. "I'm going to bed."

She couldn't get the thoughts to stop racing through her brain. A weight pressed on her. If Dad found out what she and Mom planned, he'd have a cow.

Why did her parents have to be so different? Dad was thrilled she'd invited a friend from school over to help her. If he knew the motivation behind the offer, he'd give her a tongue lashing.

Then he'd give Mom an earful as well. And Mom would give it right back. It would go back and forth for hours. Listening to them go at it sometimes could be so confusing.

Visions of the classroom swam in her head. Harper's desk sat two people in front of her. Would Lizzy be able to pull this off without someone catching her? And what if the teacher didn't see it?

The blaring alarm startled her, and her heart's rapid pattering warned her she hadn't gotten enough sleep to feel whole and healthy. She tapped the snooze option on her phone. Perhaps another fifteen minutes would make the difference.

The phone's second chime felt no better than the first, but at least her heart didn't go rapid-fire. Time to face the day.

Hot water steamed the bathroom mirror because she'd left the exhaust fan off, but she didn't care. She'd needed the heat and needling water to soothe her sleepy brain. Today would be challenging enough without being foggy brained.

By the time she arrived in the kitchen, Mary was already cleaning up the crumbs from her toast. She carried her mug to the sink and rinsed it.

"Morning." Mary chirped every morning, like a happy sparrow from a cartoon. "Ready for the big test?"

Today, of all days, she didn't want to deal with Miss Happy-Happy Joy-Joy, but here she stood. "Yeah."

Mary's head tilted to the side, and her eyes narrowed. "Looks like you didn't sleep much last night. I guess we stayed up too late."

There were no words, not at this hour. Lizzy shrugged.

Mary's eyes lit up as if the most wonderful idea had just struck her between the eyes. "Can I make you some cocoa and peanut butter toast?"

The thought of putting food into her mouth was revolting. "No thanks. I'm not feeling all that great."

Mary's eyes softened, and she reached out as if to hug her when Mom strode into the kitchen.

"I don't think Lizzy feels too good this morning," Mary said.

Lizzy stepped out of range of the oncoming hug.

Mom glanced at Lizzy, and her eyes hardened. "I'm sure she's just nervous about the test. She'll be fine."

That look meant suck it up, buttercup.

«»

The teacher walked across the front of the room, counting out test papers for each row. As soon as he handed a small stack to the first person in the row, each student took one and passed the rest back. Once everyone had a set of questions in front of them, he said, "Begin."

Then he sat at his desk as the classroom became quiet. Only the scratching of pencils on paper and flipping of pages dared interrupt.

After she'd answered half the questions, it was now or never.

If she didn't act, she'd lose her resolve. Mom sent her a text message before class started.

Don't forget.

Forget? How could she? It was all she could think about. All her mom talked about for the past week when they were alone together.

She pushed down hard on her pencil tip until the end snapped. The lead tip flipped into the air and landed in the girl's hair in front of her.

The sound had been just loud enough to catch the teacher's attention. She held her pencil up, and his quizzical stare became a nod.

Standing, she walked to the pencil sharpener in the corner, palming a note she'd pulled out of her pocket.

On her return route, she dropped the note on the teacher's desk.

No one looked up. She heaved a grateful sigh.

As she regained her seat, a glance showed the teacher reading the note. He made eye contact.

She nodded, then turned her attention to the papers in front of her.

It wouldn't do to look, so she watched him through the corner of her eye. He moved through the room, eventually hovering over Harper's desk.

He bent down and picked up a paper on top of Harper's bag.

She knew what it was, and the teacher's narrowing eyes said he knew as well.

He tapped Harper on the shoulder and motioned for her to follow him.

As he strode to the door, Harper rose from her desk and looked around the room as if searching for something she couldn't see. The teacher opened the classroom door and motioned for Harper to exit. She did, and he followed.

Beyond the door's window, the teacher's eyes flared, and he shook the paper he'd picked up in Harper's face. The girl's face mottled red, and she shook her head while his eyes hardened. He pointed down the hallway, and Harper fled.

Bull's-eye.

6

Chapter Six

The school buzzed with the news. Lizzy's head throbbed under the barrage of words Ava continued to vomit.

"I still can't believe it." It had to be the tenth time Ava repeated the phrase to her and Mary. "Cheating. Harper. The two words don't go together."

"We don't know she cheated for sure." Mary continued to stick up for the accused while every other person in the hallway discussed Harper's guilt as if it were a forgone conclusion. "It's probably just a misunderstanding."

Ava pivoted and walked backward so she could talk face-to-face. "Misunderstanding? How do you accidentally leave your study notes on your book bag, facing up, during a test?"

The air quotes Ava used to emphasize the word flipped into upraised palms.

Lizzy couldn't take another word as she massaged her aching temple. "Can we please stop talking about this?"

Mary's eyes slanted toward her. "Maybe you should go see the nurse. Do you get migraines?"

Ava's gleeful prance paused, which stopped their progression in the middle of the hallway. "I just realized something. If they suspend Harper for cheating, they'll also kick her out of her president role. That means they'll promote you to president."

Ava's hand covered the O of her gaping mouth. Her eyes went wide.

Precisely what the plan had been. The strategy was working perfectly. Or was it?

If the ruse was working so well, why was a drummer striking up this wicked rhythm in her head? Wasn't this what she wanted?

She couldn't release the memory of Harper's face—confusion followed by tears—while the teacher scolded her in the hallway. Whispers of the scandal flew through the school faster than the football team could eat a pizza. Everyone theorized why she'd cheat on a test and risk her reputation.

Of course, the fall of a teacher's pet was the best scandal the school had to feast on in weeks. The victim's status added additional hot sauce to the fare.

Nausea tag teamed the thrumming in her head now. Great. Maybe it was a migraine. She'd never had one before, but this was her first attempt at undoing another human. What she expected was exhilaration, but what she felt was creepy.

The cryptic text to her mother confirmed her complicity. Mom's good-job response felt anything but.

As she ruminated on the issue, students streamed into the last class. A pair of girls entered the room and sat in the row ahead of her. Their stage whispers drew the attention of all within hearing range.

One girl shook perfectly coifed blond hair around her contrasting black face mask. "I saw her crying her eyes out when her mother picked her up."

The second girl performed a textbook eye roll. "Can you blame her? I heard she got an F on the test and got suspended for a week. They say she even got grounded for a month."

Lizzy winced.

The first girl pulled her mask down and leaned toward her friend, a wicked grin in place. "She's going to lose the class president's role for sure."

By the time Dad picked her and Mary up, Lizzy's head threatened to explode. "You all right?"

Though spoken quietly, the sound reverberated between her ears as she settled into her seat. Lizzy closed her eyes and leaned against the cool window. "I don't feel so good."

"I think it's a migraine," Mary softly added. "She hasn't been feeling well all day."

A soft hand touched her shoulder from behind. Wasn't that just like Mary to show compassion? What would the response be if Mary knew the source of the pain?

As they walked into the house, Mom was unpacking dinner from Minnie's. It smelled like the fried chicken special. Although one of Lizzy's favorites, the scent was revolting today.

"I'm going to bed." She tried to move through the kitchen as fast as possible. "Can't eat."

Mom's voice followed as the need to get to her bedroom became urgent. "Wait, what…"

She barely made it to the toilet in time. Though she'd not been able to eat lunch, something in her stomach needed to come up. The yellow-green hues indicated bile was all her body had to toss back up. Disgusting.

A knock at the door interrupted her body's shenanigans.

"Honey, are you okay? Can I come in?"

"No." She wasn't sure how she felt about Dad being the one

to ask the question. "Don't come in. I need to clean up and go to bed."

His compassion would undo her. No doubt about it. He couldn't know what she'd done, and right now, if he put his arms around her in that warm embrace of his, she'd spill it all.

"I'll send your mom in to help."

"No. I'm fine. I just want to go to bed."

Mom's plotting wouldn't stop. Normally, Lizzy would be all about learning the ins and outs of getting ahead, but she'd had enough for today. Maybe she wasn't cut from the same cloth as her mother. But she wasn't the huggee-feely of her father either.

Who was she? What did she stand for? She thought she knew the answer, but now, she wasn't sure.

Her head ached as she dragged herself off the floor and brushed the awful taste out of her mouth.

Once she'd stripped off her clothes, she slid on her favorite bedtime sleepwear—one of her father's cast-off T-shirts. When he'd given it to her, it had hung almost to the floor. Now it fell just below her knees.

She'd felt so safe in it back then, like he was with her, protecting her from nightmares. It smelled of him for an entire week before Mom washed it the first time. Now, as she crawled into bed, the shirt reminded her of simpler times when she could allow such simple notions to comfort her. Life was much too complicated for a piece of cloth to soothe it all away.

The tap on the door was so quiet she almost thought she'd imagined it. She opened her eyes. Huh. The sun was setting. So, she'd slept for at least an hour or two.

Her head didn't ache as it had earlier, but she still didn't want to face the world. Rolling over, she settled in to sleep some more.

This time, the tap was more urgent. "Lizzy, are you awake?"

Perhaps if she ignored her, Mary would go away.

Instead, the doorknob turned, and the hall light shone through the crack of the opening door. "Lizzy, are you awake? Can I talk to you?"

Her cousin wasn't going to give up.

She breathed out a sigh, then sat up. "What's up?"

Mary closed the door behind her and tiptoed over to the bed and sat cross-legged at Lizzy's feet, the fluffy white duvet billowing around her. "I was hoping you were awake. Can we just talk for a bit? Or maybe I could talk if you're too tired. I–I just need someone to be close to right now."

As the last words wobbled, Lizzy positioned herself against her headboard. "You, okay?"

A laugh-huff-sob came out as Mary wrapped her fingers in her nightshirt and twisted, then untwisted the hem. "Not really."

Great. Just spectacular. Lizzy so couldn't deal with people's emotions. Why couldn't Mary have gone to Dad? He was a pro at this sort of thing.

What would he say now? "Do you want to talk about it?"

Mary stared at her wringing hands and shrugged—then nodded. "I guess so."

The pause was excruciating. A second felt like a minute… two minutes? Should she say something? What?

Mary ended the word drought. "I miss my mom, my friends back home, and the mission."

Oh, that was it. Just homesickness. "I'm sorry."

Mary's eyes went wide. "Oh no. It's not that you and your family haven't been wonderful. And your friends are so sweet.

It's just not the same as being home."

Well, now what? She'd said she was sorry. What came after that?

This was why she didn't have friends. She didn't know how to *do* friendship. Never had. That's why Mom's way of life seemed so much more appealing than Dad's. He always knew what to say—always had a shoulder to cry on and a comforting word to share.

Mom was the "suck it up, buttercup."

Caring about others, helping others, wasn't straightforward. *This* wasn't easy.

Her cousin lowered her head again and remained silent, other than an occasional sniffle.

Lizzy reached over to the bedside table and pulled two tissues out of the box on it. She handed them to Mary without a word.

Words. What would Dad say now? "Can I do something to help?"

A shake of Mary's head came first. But a beat later, she let out a deep sigh. "Can I just hang out in here for a while? It's too lonely in my room. I could just read. I'll be quiet."

As her cousin's need tugged at her, Lizzy twisted the knob on the lamp, and a circle of light fell over the head of the bed. She slid to the opposite side and crawled back down under the covers. "Just switch the light off when you're done reading. Okay?"

"Thanks." A soggy response accompanied the shuffling of Mary's transition to the headboard. "I appreciate it."

Lizzy closed her eyes, prepared to chase the sandman once more. "No problem."

It was silent in the room for a beat or two. Then Mary whispered. "Lizzy?"

Ugh. Would this night never end? She just wanted to sleep, for crying out loud. "Yes?"

"Do you have a book I can borrow?"

«»

The next morning's alarm woke Lizzy with a start. She hadn't moved from the position she'd fallen asleep in. When she rolled over, Mary was gone.

After she finished her morning shower and dressed, she found her cousin at the kitchen island, dressed and ready to go to school, coffee in hand and toast half eaten on her plate.

Mary pivoted on her stool and smiled as Lizzy entered the room. "We're out of bread. But there are waffles in the freezer if you'd like me to pop one into the toaster."

No signs of the previous night's distress remained. She looked as calm and put together as always.

Tempted to just go with the cocoa, Lizzy changed her mind when her stomach growled, reminding her she hadn't eaten the previous day. "Thanks. I'll get it, though. I'm famished."

Mary popped off the island stool. "I'll make cocoa while you get the waffles. It's the least I can do after keeping you up late last night."

Lizzy wanted to forget the previous night. Today, the world seemed to realign itself. Worrying about friendships and feelings weakened her yesterday. Look at what it had done to her body. The crushing headache, the nausea, and the vomiting—all because she cared what happened to Harper.

Then she'd lost sleep galore because Mary wanted a friend. Who needed that? She was much better off on her island, moving people around like chess pieces on a board.

That made more sense. Detachment. All business. Just like Mom. Much less messy. Back to reality. Time to see if her plan worked.

Chapter Seven

The walkway looked barren compared to the norm when Lizzy and Mary arrived at the school. Even though few students milled around outside the building, a line snaked out of the entrance.

Normally, the scanners weren't so backed up.

They joined the lineup. But it wasn't the security check taking time. Instead, the temperature checks were back in place.

"I can't believe we're checking temperatures again." Lizzy rolled her eyes at Mary. "I thought we were past all of this."

Mary's gaze darted between the lines and Lizzy, unable to settle. "What if it's going to get bad here, like it is back in Honduras?"

As they drew closer to the foyer, Mrs. Burns patrolled the queue, ensuring compliance. "Mr. Parker, pull that mask over your nose. This isn't a game."

Girls giggled as the administrative assistant turned away from the boy, and he made an inappropriate gesture to her back.

When the boy in front of Lizzy reached the temperature scanner, it blasted red and issued loud and rapid beeps. The nurse manning the machine directed the boy to a separate area where a group of students waited.

Having made it through the health checkpoint, they proceeded to their lockers and then to the classroom where Ava waited for them. She sprang out of her seat as soon as they entered. "Did you hear? A bunch of students left school early yesterday, sick. I heard even more called off today. I think a new variant is going around."

Students trickled in, but by the time the first bell rang, less than half the classroom was present.

The overhead speaker buzzed to life, and the principal began the morning announcements. "Good morning, everyone. By now you've all noticed we're missing several of your classmates today."

Everyone looked around the room as if it wasn't already painfully obvious how few were in attendance.

The principal continued. "Some students who left school ill yesterday are reporting they tested positive for the variant. As you are already aware, we reinstated the temperature checks. Because quite a few are running fevers this morning, we're only going to run classes for half the day. I'm afraid we're going back to virtual classrooms for now."

A low buzz filled the room.

"We'll line the buses up soon to return everyone home. Those who need to make alternative arrangements are free to use their cell phones today to coordinate with their families."

Backpacks unzipped. Phones chimed to life. Quick fingers texted parents the news while the principal continued with the morning messages. Few students seemed engaged with anything besides their devices.

Lizzy got her own out and texted her parents about needing

a ride home.

The announcements ended. Then the room's intercom buzzed to life once more, catching everyone's attention. "Mr. Evans, please send Lizzy Tilbrook to the office."

Her eyebrows shot up as she made eye contact with the teacher.

"Will do." Mr. Evans jerked a thumb toward the door while holding out a hall pass. "You heard the summons, Miss Tilbrook. Don't keep them waiting."

"What's going on?" Ava's hissed under her breath while at least three other students stared.

Lizzy stood and shrugged. "I have no clue, but I guess I'm going to find out." She pulled her book bag onto her shoulders and started toward the door, accepting the hall pass on her way out. "I'll catch up with you as soon as I can."

Why had the principal summoned her? Had they figured out what she'd done to Harper? Her stomach roiled, and she tasted acid at the back of her mouth.

Mrs. Burns looked up from her desk as Lizzy stepped into the office. "Principal Stover is waiting for you in his office."

That didn't sound good.

Her feet somehow continued to move her body forward, past Mrs. Burns's catty cubby, even though her heart wanted to run in the opposite direction.

The buzz of the phone in her hand paused her progress just before she reached the principal's door. Dad's text was brief.

I'll pick you up at noon.

Too bad he wasn't there now. Then she'd have an excuse to put off this meeting.

"Go on in, dear," Mrs. Burns said.

Lizzy crept across the threshold. Mr. Stover sat at his desk, typing away on his laptop. He looked up, peering at her over the top of his reading glasses. His left hand unhooked the spectacles braced on his ears while his right gestured toward a guest chair. "Have a seat, Miss Tilbrook."

Two chairs rested in front of his desk. They looked heavy, made of dark wood with a leather finish. It might as well have been an electric chair for all the reluctance she felt at sitting on it. Did he know what she'd done? Was she about to get called out? Suspended?

What would her parents say? Disappointment and anger from Dad were a given. Mom's anger wouldn't be because of what she'd done, but because she'd been clumsy enough to get caught.

"Miss Tilbrook." Principal Stover raised an eyebrow and pointed at the seat on her right. "The chair won't bite, I assure you. Please sit."

Heat flushed her face as she sat. "Yes, sir."

"There has been a bit of an incident." He formed a temple with his hands. "I'm afraid circumstances have disqualified Miss Jones for the class president role she held. Therefore, since you're vice president, I am officially promoting you to the president's position."

The release of breath she hadn't realized she was holding allowed her to take in some desperately needed fresh air. How should she react? What would he expect from someone who wasn't fully aware of Harper's innocence?

She so badly wanted to fidget. Her body itched to move, but best not to look guilty.

"I'm sorry to hear Harper won't be able to function as president anymore. Of course, I'll do all I can to help. Anything you need."

He responded with a brief nod, followed by a shuffling of papers on his desk. "I've got a list of the projects Miss Harper indicated she had in process." He handed her one sheet with a bullet-pointed list. "Give her a few days to adjust to the transition, but she said she'd be happy to answer questions."

Unable to grasp the meaning of any sentences, Lizzy pretended to read through the list. The letters swam in front of her eyes, refusing to settle into comprehensive thoughts.

She needed out of this office and away from his prying eyes. "Yes, sir. I'll connect with her if I need to."

His gaze seemed to peer into her soul, reading her thoughts. Did he know? If he did, could he prove it? Did the teacher suspect?

"I have nothing else for you, so unless you have questions, you may return to your class schedule."

She popped up off the chair as if ejected from a fighter jet going down in flames. "Yes, sir. Thank you, sir."

Class had already begun by the time she caught up with Ava and Mary. She slipped into her chair after handing the teacher her hall pass.

Ava's eyebrows rose into the obvious question. *What's up?*

"Later," Lizzy mouthed.

The class was over before she could settle her thoughts enough to listen to the lesson. She tapped the assignment notes into her laptop before closing it and filing out into the hallway.

Ava and Mary waited just outside the door.

"Well?" Ava was the first to assault her. "What happened?"

"Is everything okay?" Mary followed with her own thoughts. "Is there a problem at home?"

What was this? A verbal firing squad? "Everything is fine. Principal Stover just made me the class president. He disqualified Harper."

Ava's eyes grew to the size of quarters. "Oh, wow! This is huge!"

Mary seemed to struggle with her reaction. "Congratulations?"

The smile Lizzy forced in place felt weak, probably not even visible beyond the mask. That was most likely the source of her cousin's confusion. Lizzy pushed harder to brighten her eyes, shoving the smile into them. "Thanks. I've got a list of projects to take care of now—stuff Harper started but didn't get to finish."

Ava bounced in front of her, walking backward as they advanced down the hallway. "You know I'll help you. Mary will too, right?"

Mary's confused expression resolved into a confirmation. "Of course, I will. Anything to help."

The short day ended before Lizzy could sort through her emotions. She hoped they wouldn't talk about it on the drive home, but when she got in Dad's truck, he had the radio on, listening to the news intently.

The news anchor was discussing the current outbreak with a representative from the CDC. "The variant is hitting multiple cities simultaneously, so we don't think it's a new strain. Our experts think the virus is reactivating in people who had it before."

Dad reached across the front seat to squeeze her shoulder.

The CDC representative continued. "The hypothesis we're going on is those who have symptoms now, who didn't have the variant previously, probably had infections but were asymptomatic. This reactivation is bringing on the full-blown version."

The news anchor's response crowded out thoughts of her deception. "Doctor, hospitals are already filling again. Are they prepared for this new wave of patients?"

The exhale of breath came through the truck's speakers as the CDC person responded. "I certainly hope so. Hospitals are short-staffed because of the number of people who left the workforce during the pandemic. Pray for those who are still in our healthcare facilities. They're going to need it."

«»

When they pulled up to the house, an RV waited in their driveway. A gigantic red bow covered the vehicle's hood.

That's right. Dad's birthday was next week.

They hurried out of the truck as soon as they'd parked behind the RV. The garage door rose while they wandered around the camper's elegant exterior, and Mom rattled a set of keys as she joined them at the hood.

She handed Dad the key and hugged him. "Happy early birthday, Dan."

Dad opened his mouth, then closed it with a huge grin. His gaze never left the RV as he stroked the hood. "It's the expensive one with solar panels and a hybrid engine. How can we afford this?"

She opened the driver's door and waved him into the seat. "I got my bonus. You've been dreaming about traveling the country for years. Life is short. It's time you started living your dream. At least on vacations."

That was his long-held desire. He'd always wanted to drive through every state in the continental United States. This had to be the nicest gift her mom had ever given him. Mom truly did love Dad, even if it didn't show all the time.

His eyes got misty as he sat in the driver's seat and ran a hand over the dashboard. His next words sounded moist. "Thank you."

Mom beamed, hands on hips while he inspected the cockpit of his new toy. "Nothing's stopping us from taking it for a trip soon since the girls' classes are virtual again."

The words washed over Dad as if she'd thrown a bucket of cold water on his fire of enthusiasm. He frowned, stepped out of the driver's seat, and closed the door behind him. Next, he snugged Mom into a hug. "Thank you so much. I can't wait to give it a spin. But we may want to wait a week to see how this new wave of variant cases affects the world."

Mom scoffed with a roll of her eyes. "They're making a big deal out of nothing. This country is unstoppable. Let's plan our trip. Where do you want to go first?"

The rest of the evening, Mom pushed Dad to make plans. Why did she need to push at him so much? This was supposed to be a gift, and she treated it like a task he had to accomplish.

By eight o'clock, Lizzy couldn't take Mom's verbal poking any longer and escaped to her bedroom.

After she completed her assignments for school the next day, she climbed into bed, book in hand, to read herself to sleep. But she couldn't concentrate. She'd read the same paragraph at least three times and still didn't know what it said.

What she'd done to Harper wouldn't let go.

Her cell phone buzzed, alerting her to a text message. She picked up the device and saw a message from Harper.

"I heard Principal Stover gave you the president's position. I hope you're happy now. I know it was you."

8

Chapter Eight

Morning came, whether or not Lizzy was ready for it. After a sleepless night, she decided it was a not-ready-for-it kind of day.

She hadn't responded to Harper's text. What could she say? No matter how she responded, there would be a permanent record of it. Harper could use any text or voice mail against her on social networking sites. On and on it would go.

If she replied, she'd need a calculated response. This was a problem to discuss with Mom, but she needed to bring it up when Mary wasn't around.

She slogged through her morning ablutions, desperate for an energy kick. Perhaps a sugar rush from some hot cocoa would do the trick. Once more, she wished she could get past the bitterness of coffee to claim the caffeine buzz.

Mary's plate held only crumbs when Lizzy walked into the kitchen. The rich scent of coffee surrounded her. Her cousin looked up when Lizzy came in, then became enthralled with the bottom of her mug. Lizzy made her way to the refrigerator. "Morning."

The silent response thickened the air.

She pulled a mug from the rack and a packet of cocoa mix from the pantry. Since when did Mary not respond? "Everything all right?"

Mary's eyes connected, then veered away. "Have you been on Snapchat yet this morning?"

What a strange question. "No. Why? Should I?"

After taking a sip from her mug, Mary set it down. "You need to see what Harper is saying."

A chill ran down Lizzy's spine, and a knot tightened her belly. Harper wouldn't. She didn't have any proof, did she? What could she have?

Lizzy set everything on the marble counter and wiggled her cell out of her back pocket. Her hands shook, uncooperative and clumsy, as she signed into the phone and brought up the app.

There it was—for all the world to see.

Harper's post was short and bitter.

Trust no one. I thought I had a friend to help me study for a test. Instead, I fell for a skank who cares for only herself. Got me kicked out with a lie. Enjoy the president's role. You've earned it.

Even though she never called out Lizzy by name, everyone would know who Harper blamed. Lizzy's clammy hands could no longer hold the phone steady. Dropping the device to the counter, she lowered her head and took deep breaths to slow her racing heart.

Mary rose from her barstool, went to the sink, and rinsed her mug. After she placed it in the dishwasher, she turned to Lizzy. "You set her up, didn't you? You planted the answer sheet so the teacher would assume she was cheating." Mary crossed her arms. Her frown deepened. "I heard you and Aunt Jen talking about Harper. But I never thought you'd go this far. How could you?"

There were no words. Lizzy's brain fogged over, and her tongue froze to the roof of her mouth.

Not one thought coalesced into speech.

So, she shoved her hands into her pockets and stared at the floor, defeated.

"I'm calling Harper to apologize for you." Mary walked toward her room. "For this whole family."

Lizzy couldn't think past the repeated buzzes, beeps, and other notifications now blowing up her phone as it shimmied on the counter.

Now what? Where did she go from here? She needed to talk to Mom.

Where was Mom? She was always up by now. Perhaps she was still getting dressed. Even if Dad was around, Lizzy needed Mom and her advice. This had gone way beyond keeping Dad out of the loop.

She headed toward the master bedroom, calling out. "Mom?"

The door to their room opened, and Dad slipped out. He shut the door behind him with an almost imperceptible click. His hand reached up to the mask covering his face and pulled it down. "Mom's not feeling well this morning. She came down with a fever last night."

She couldn't remember the last time her mother had been sick. Mom didn't even catch colds.

"Is she okay?" Lizzy advanced toward her father.

But he thrust out an arm to stop her. "We gave her a variant test. She's positive."

It was the first time anyone in the family had been ill since the whole mess began. She'd assumed they were all immune by now.

Mom was healthy. She rarely went to the doctor because she never got sick. Regular exercise kept her slim enough to fit into her wedding dress after over twenty years of marriage. How many other moms could say that?

"Are you taking her to the doctor? To the hospital?"

"No, honey." He shook his head. "The hospitals are full. I called the doctor, and he's going to call in something for her to the pharmacy. I'm heading there now."

What should she do? There had to be some way to help. "Should I make her something to eat? Some coffee?"

He wrapped his arms around her and pulled her to his chest. "She's sleeping. Let's let her rest."

She needed something to focus on. "What do you need me to do?"

Releasing her, he headed toward the garage. "Why don't you bring your laptop out to the dining room to work today? If your mom wakes up and needs something, you'll be around to help."

She nodded.

He continued. "Remember to wear your mask if you go into the bedroom. I can't imagine we won't all come down with it now that it's in the household, but we're going to do our best to stay well."

The rest of the day was a blur of information overload. Ava texted, PM'd, and left voice mail messages—none of which Lizzy responded to.

Other students shared Harper's post, causing it to go viral. That was that. The entire school knew what she'd been accused of. Memes of her face with a red slash through it popped up on every social media platform, reposted over and over.

It appeared the entire student body stood behind Harper, backing her up. Her popularity went beyond a pretty face. She'd developed genuine friendships with the other students. Even Mary bonded with her in the short time she'd been at the school.

The only person who might still be in her corner was Ava, but Lizzy was too antsy to look at the messages from her supposed BFF. What if she'd turned against her as well? The only person she'd have left would be her mother, and Mom wasn't even well enough to leave her bedroom.

Dad arrived home early that afternoon. Dark circles under his eyes emphasized the tightness of his mouth and jaw. "Sorry I was gone so long. What I thought would be a quick trip to the pharmacy became a game of seek and find. The pharmacies are running out of medications. No one expected a wave to hit so suddenly."

He raised the small white bag above his head as if it were an Olympic medal. "But I got what she needed at the sixth store. Waited in line for an hour to get it."

"I haven't seen Mom yet today." Fidgety, Lizzy glanced at the bedroom door as if waiting for her mother to pop out at any moment. "I'm worried, Dad. I tapped on the door a few times, but she never responded."

She'd cracked the door open an inch and peered in as well, but Mom didn't even move on the bed when Lizzy whispered her name.

"I'll check on her." Dad lowered the white bag, took a glass from the cabinet, and filled it with water from the refrigerator door. "I'm sure she's just sleeping. Where's Mary?"

Now wasn't the time to go into the school drama. "She's

working in her bedroom. It's easier when we're not overlapping each other's virtual classes."

"I'll let you get back to that." He kissed the top of her head as he passed by on his way to the master bedroom. "Maybe you could help with supper later?"

She responded to his retreating back. "Sure."

Something wasn't right. A tingling sensation of foreboding had her body vibrating.

She catapulted out of the chair when her father yelled from the bedroom. "Call 911!"

Fingers fumbled as she struggled to turn her cell back on. She'd shut it off to silence the constant notifications. Now she couldn't bring the phone back to life soon enough.

It felt like hours before a signal came up and she could dial.

A robotic voice said, "911—what is your emergency?"

"We need help, please—help us!"

«»

She owned nothing black. Never liked how it made her look—pale, like a vampire in an old movie. The dress she now wore hung loose on her frame.

Unfortunately, Mom's wardrobe was the only place to find clothes. The stores had to shut down because of the number of people who'd called in sick.

It had been so sudden. How could Mom have progressed from feisty to feverish and then gone in only two days? The ambulances had been so backed up with calls they said it would be hours before they could come. Dad had gathered Mom into his arms and put her into the truck. She was gone by the time he carried her into the emergency room, and they couldn't revive her.

By the next morning, the rest of them were sick in bed.

Thankfully, none of them were as sick as Mom.

Now, two weeks later, they'd recovered enough to pick up Mom's cremated remains to say their goodbyes formally.

Perhaps they were fortunate to have gotten her ashes back. So many died within a few short days. The bodies piled up. Only the first wave of corpses made their way to funeral homes for proper handling. They stuck the rest in refrigerator trucks and hospital morgues. Better than the streets. Though if it continued much longer, that would be the fate of the next wave.

A knock on her bedroom door brought her out of musings.

"You ready?" Dad's thin frame had grown gaunt from the illness. He looked like a teen who'd borrowed his father's too-big suit. "It's time to go."

"Coming."

She wandered toward her door with no desire to face the day ahead. As she came out of her room, Mary stepped into the hallway. Though pale, she'd gotten through the illness with minor weight loss. She'd even cared for Lizzy and her father as they recovered.

Mary pulled her into an embrace. "I'm sorry. We'll get through this together."

Lizzy nodded, but words were more difficult to come by. What was there to say? It just hurt, everywhere and in every way.

They drove to the cemetery where they'd buried her grandparents, Mom's parents. Lizzy sat in the front passenger seat, clinging to the small box containing her mother's ashes.

At least, the cemetery was close enough that the trip wouldn't use much gas. Most of the gas stations had run out of fuel. The National Guard brought in some supplies, but getting the limited quantities available remained difficult. They wouldn't be traveling much until the world fixed its supply chain issues.

When they arrived, they sat in the truck as if all three shared the same thought, though no one put words to it. If they stepped out of the vehicle, they'd have to say goodbye.

It felt like hours passed before Dad sucked in a deep breath and opened his door. He went to the back door, helped Mary out, then came around to the passenger door, and opened it for Lizzy. He held out his hand for her, and she clasped it as if he were saving her from drowning.

Could you suffocate from the world closing in around you?

Exiting the vehicle, she hugged the box tight to her chest. After she stood solidly on her feet, he went to the back of the truck and removed a shovel.

The sun shone bright and clear as they walked toward her grandparents' headstones. They stood in front of the graves, as if unsure how to proceed.

The cemetery held smatterings of other mourners. One woman kneeled under a tree in a grove of children's headstones, sobbing as she clung to a stuffed bear.

Dad dug a hole between the two headstones and laid the shovel aside. He and Mary put their arms around Lizzy's shoulders.

"It's time," he said.

But she couldn't move. The ground was no place for her mom.

Mary lowered her head until wisps of her bun tickled Lizzy's forehead. "Father, we don't understand why you've allowed this disease to take Aunt Jen, but we're so grateful you have her safe now. Tell her we love her and can't wait to see her again. Amen."

Dad squeezed Lizzy tight. "Amen."

She mouthed the word, but no sound escaped her swollen throat.

The hole seemed to move to her, instead of her to the hole. She dropped to her knees.

Lowering the box into the ground, she whispered, "Bye, Mom."

Chapter Nine

A mental fog surrounded Lizzy as she stumbled through the next week. The world fell apart around her. It wasn't only the loss of her mother, but normalcy faltered more with each passing day.

A bouquet wilted on the dining room table. Dad's best friend from work dropped it off a week ago. With no florists open, he'd picked the flowers from his wife's garden. That was it—nothing else from anyone to memorialize her mother's passing. Not even a peep from Mom's friend Diane.

Mom always said friends weren't important. People were resources. But resources don't care if you die, especially if you're one of the millions gone within days of each other.

Even Ava hadn't sent as much as a text message. But then again, the paper wasn't exactly posting obituaries any longer. There weren't enough people still working at the paper to report on something as common as a death. The reporters spent most of their time discussing options for those who had no food.

Lizzy sat before the television in the game room, nibbling at dry cereal. It would be so nice to have cold milk to splash over it, but everything spoiled when the power went out for three days in a row last week. No matter. She couldn't handle more than a nibble here and there, anyway.

She'd tuned the television to the news. Dad joined her on the couch and pulled her into an embrace. His body warmed her as she laid her head on his shoulder.

He kissed the top of her head. "Anything positive going on in the world?"

With a shake of her head, she buried herself in his side. "It's hard to watch because they don't have cameramen working. It's like watching shaky YouTube videos."

The newscaster, a woman in a poorly pressed suit, held her camera phone to film herself. Her voice crackled from the speakers. "The electric grid is no longer stable. There aren't enough people to troubleshoot line breaks and other issues. FEMA's instructions are to expect intermittent power outages for the foreseeable future."

There was no switch from the on-view presenter to the person back at the studio, but a male voice spoke while the on-screen newscaster listened. "Debra, did FEMA indicate how they planned to get the grid into a stable position in the future?"

The woman nodded and stared at the floor as if there were a delay in the transmission and she waited for the question to reach her ears. After a long pause, she made eye contact with the camera on her phone. "The FEMA representative said they have assigned all remaining military personnel to various defense positions, Bob. Once they determine the country is secure, they'll begin allocation of resources to infrastructure. Until then, it will be up to the local governments to care for their communities as best they can."

Lizzy's stomach ached from more than the emptiness it endured since the funeral. The cereal she'd munched on earlier tasted like sawdust.

Mary wandered in and sat on Dad's other side. "Internet's down again. I only had it for a few minutes this morning, but I saw an email from Mom. She's on her way here." She wrapped her arm around Lizzy's shoulders. "Rumor is the military was evacuating Americans. She might catch one of the last flights but said she'd catch any transportation she could."

"What are we going to do, Dad?" Lizzy looked into her father's eyes, desperate to see strength. "It's all falling apart."

The set of his eyes dared her to doubt him. "Are you kidding me? We're going to be fine." His firm squeeze told her he'd be strong enough for both of them. "As soon as your aunt Rebecca gets here, we're going to make a plan as a family."

A tear formed, but she swiped it away. If he could be strong, so could she. "What kind of plan?"

He rubbed her shoulder with a brisk motion, then stood to face her and Mary. "It's time to figure out our food situation." He picked up the remote and switched the TV off. "Time to learn how to grow and preserve. We can't rely on the government to feed us."

The empty ache in her stomach morphed into a grumble. Perhaps she should have forced more food down before it spoiled. Dad tried to convince her, but her stomach clenched every time she contemplated eating.

"We've still got canned goods in the pantry." Mary piped up then. "Don't you think that'll hold us over until things get moving again?"

He shook his head, crossed his arms over his chest, and paced.

Three steps to the wall, then three back. He probably didn't realize he was doing it. "We need to get out of the city. Your mother's birthday gift is just what we need to travel. Thankfully, Mom stocked it with propane and other supplies before this happened. If we're careful, it should last us a little while."

The tightening in her chest clamped down harder.

A gasp drew her gaze to Mary's hand covering her mouth. Her cousin's eyes were wide. "Do you really think we should leave the city? Won't people come into the city for help? FEMA will bring food in. Won't they?"

Dad came back to them and kneeled, placing his hands on theirs. "The entire country—no, the *world*—lost too many people at one time. This isn't something we're going to move past in a few months. Maybe we won't recover for years. There isn't enough food in storage to feed everyone. We'll need to fend for ourselves."

Mary scooted forward. "It's like this event equalized the world. We're all poor now. It's not exactly back to the Stone Age, but we're set back to preindustrial times."

With a spring, Lizzy got off the couch and strode the length of the room before spinning back to her father. "Can't we stay here? This is home."

His eyes softened, and a sad smile settled on his lips. "I know it is. But Mom's not here anymore, and home will be wherever we are together."

«»

Lies. The photo album Lizzy'd perused for the past hour was full of them. Mom and her poolside on vacation, Dad obviously behind the camera. Then Dad's arm around her on the airboat ride when Mom had been the photographer.

Why hadn't she ever seen it before? There weren't any

pictures of the three of them together. Would it have been that difficult to ask a passerby to take the camera for a moment?

That wasn't how their family rolled. The constant tug-of-war her parents played exhausted her, and she hadn't realized how much until now.

The tap at the door pulled her out of her head. Mary gave her a sad smile. "Can I come in?"

With a nod, Lizzy scooted over, patting the bed beside her. Mary sat and slid her legs onto the crisp white bedspread, leaning into Lizzy's side.

She rested her head on Mary's shoulder, then pointed to the open album. "I'd never realized it before, but I don't have a picture of myself with my parents."

"I'm so sorry. I know how difficult it is to miss a parent."

How could she have been so stupid? Mary'd lived without a father for years. He'd abandoned his family while they were on a mission trip. If Lizzy remembered correctly, Dad said Mary's father lost faith in what they'd been doing. Just ran off with another woman, back to the States, and never looked back.

Lizzy closed the album. "Your mom is so strong. I'd forgotten about your dad. Do you miss him?"

Mary shrugged, then smiled. "Honestly, it's been so long since he left that I barely remember him. Mom misses him sometimes, though."

Laughter bubbled up, uncontrolled.

Eyeing her as if she'd lost her mind, Mary barked out an answering giggle. "What's so funny about that?"

Lizzy wiped a tear from her eye. Maybe she *was* losing her mind. "I was just thinking about Mom. She wouldn't have missed Dad. At least I don't think she would have. Honestly, I don't think she ever needed anyone."

Mary pulled her legs up to sit cross-legged, facing Lizzy. "But what about you? You've always kept people at arm's length yourself. Don't you want someone to be close to? To share your secrets with?"

With her cousin's eyes so intent, she must be trying to dig into Lizzy's soul. She ducked her head, not comfortable baring her heart.

"Honestly, I'd love to have what you have. Real friends. It looks amazing from the outside looking in."

Mary's bright smile shone like a lighthouse beacon. "One of my favorite Bible verses talks about friendship. It's in Ecclesiastes. It talks about how two people together is better than one person alone."

Lizzy squirmed closer to Mary. She'd never even heard of that part of the Bible. Of course, she'd never opened the book herself, so just about anything could be in it.

"It goes on to say that two people can defend against an attacker better than one person alone. Also that a cord with three strings is much harder to break. To me, that means the more friends I have, the stronger I'll be. Does that make sense?"

It did. Mary was the strongest person she knew. The bonds she grew everywhere she went made her even tougher. Lizzy could only imagine how much deeper her own family's love would have been if Mom and Dad supported each other the way Mary backed her friends.

«»

Lizzy's feet hurt from the five-mile walk and standing for hours in the queue. Mary fidgeted beside her, waiting for their share of the dry goods the National Guard was handing out from the back of semitrailers. Pinto beans and corn meal were the primary giveaway, but she'd seen some canned goods pulling at the bottoms of bags as people walked away.

Dad was in another line across the mall parking lot, a lottery for fuel. Mary'd said a prayer for them before leaving the house—for safety and provision. Those words took on new meaning as guardsmen held rifles and scanned the crowd.

"If it gets much hotter, my shoes are going to melt into the asphalt." Mary stretched her tired legs. "But we've made progress. Probably only another hour, and it'll be our turn."

Lizzy craned to look up the line, then back behind them. They had gotten farther than she realized. "I hope they aren't out by the time we get there."

Shouts from the front of the line rang out, and several military personnel faced the ruckus. Someone screamed, and the front of the tidy line turned into a jumble. While some ran away from the trailer doors, guardsmen ran in.

Unsure what to do, Lizzy froze in place. They were so close to getting food. She couldn't give up their hard-earned spot in line, but an explosion of gunfire decided for them.

Mary grabbed her arm, and they ran.

As hundreds of people scattered from the orderly line, the confusion overwhelmed her. Screams, gunshots, people fallen in front of her—it was a pandemonium of humanity, and she needed to escape.

"Wait. We've got to find Dad." She stopped, which caused Mary to jerk hard on her arm. "We can't leave him!"

Mary shook her head and pulled harder. "He'll head for the same place as us—the meeting location. We'll find him there."

Lizzy allowed her cousin to draw her farther away from the crowds toward home but continued to look back, searching for her father. "Stop. I see him."

Dad jogged toward them. The red gas can in his right hand

caused him to walk lopsided. "Go, run! Don't stop. I'll catch up."

"Come on." Another yank on her arm felt as though Mary were trying to dislodge the appendage from her shoulder. "We need to get out of here."

They took off, sprinting with all they had. Dad disappeared into the crowd.

A woman ran past, a bag heavy with food slowing her escape—too slow. A man with a handgun ran up behind the fleeing woman, hit her on the head from behind, and scooped up the food as she fell.

Lizzy's heart raced while blood ran down the woman's face as she sat up—confused by the shock of the assault.

As they approached her, Mary reached down to help the woman up. Lizzy tried to pull Mary along.

"No. We can't stop."

With a hard yank, Mary freed herself from Lizzy's grip. "This is what we're meant to do. Help me!"

Mind abuzz with the frantic movements around them, Lizzy dropped back and lifted the woman under her right shoulder, while Mary took over the left side. Though people jostled them and knocked them to the ground a few times, they managed to half-walk and half-carry the woman to the side yard of a nearby home.

They settled the woman against the house. When Lizzy stood up, blood slicked her fingertips. How could she process all that had happened? A backward glance showed people being swallowed up in the fleeing masses.

Mary separated the woman's long-sleeved shirt from her tank top. Wrapping it around the woman's head, she bunched the material over the wound and tightened it into position with the sleeves. "Are you okay, ma'am?"

Though her eyes didn't focus on either of them, the woman nodded. "I'm fine. Go. Get out of here."

A man ran up and pushed Mary aside. "I'm her husband."

He gathered the woman into his chest and cried. "I'm sorry. I saw, but I couldn't catch up."

What a relief. They wouldn't have to decide on abandoning her or making their way to meet Dad.

"Let's get out of here." Mary grabbed Lizzy's wrist once again. They ran.

And ran.

She wanted to turn back. The pain in her wrist was becoming excruciating. Mary's grasp was impossibly tight. And Lizzy's lungs might explode if she didn't stop soon. "We can't run five miles. I have to stop."

Instead of easing up, Mary jerked even harder. "You can stop when we get to the meetup spot."

They'd agreed on where to find each other once they completed their respective tasks. Dad insisted on having a set place, away from the crowds, in case things went wrong. She'd thought he was being overly cautious. Now she was grateful.

The red house with the blue shutters. They were supposed to gather here. They'd scoped it out on the way in and ensured its abandoned state. No one would see them as they slipped through the gate at the back of the wooden fence. The inside north corner was the meeting place.

She dropped to her knees and gulped air like a landed fish. Mary kneeled beside her, gasping.

It seemed like an eternal wait. Where was Dad? A creak alerted her to the gate opening once more. She put her hand on Mary's shoulder to ensure she saw the movement. Dad slid through and closed the entrance behind him. He set down the gas can and gathered them both in his arms.

Being in his arms was the best feeling in the world, and she could no longer contain her emotions. Sobs ratcheted through her as she clung to him. The world had gone insane.

10

Chapter Ten

The night reluctantly gave way to the sun as rays flickered through Lizzy's bedroom window. With no sleep to provide a break, her thoughts continued to race. Violence from the food distribution spread throughout the town last night. Gunshots in distant neighborhoods kept slumber at bay.

Dad hadn't slept much himself. He'd padded around the house. The jiggle of doorknobs and the scratch of curtains being pulled back and replaced told of his security checks throughout the night.

Whispers seeped out of Mary's room but silenced around one o'clock.

At least one of them had gotten a few winks in.

Exhaustion caused Lizzy's head to pound, but she pushed off the covers and sat up, anyway. If she remembered correctly, she had aspirin in her bathroom cabinet, so she shuffled to her door. The moment she put her hand out to twist the knob, a knock caused her heart to jump.

She yanked open the door. "I'm awake."

Dad stood in the hallway, slumped shoulders, red eyes, and wrinkled clothes from yesterday. "Just making sure you're all right. Mary's already up, cooking grits."

Lizzy nodded. "I'll get dressed and be out."

Propane—her father insisted on having the house fitted for a propane stove when they'd built it. With no natural gas available, Mom said electric would be good enough, but Dad hated cooking with electric. It was as if he'd had some sort of premonition about losing electricity. Now they could still cook, at least if there was food to prepare.

After medicating her aching head, Lizzy dressed in fresh clothing and shuffled to the kitchen to help plan for what came next.

Mary and Dad sat waiting at the kitchen island.

"Morning." Lizzy planted herself on a stool between the two, in front of a steaming bowl of grits. No cheese, no butter, and no bacon to add, so the glob looked less palatable than she'd become accustomed to. After yesterday's display of violence over the food distribution, however, gratitude seemed the only way to go.

Mary grasped her hand and nodded toward Dad. Lizzy completed the chain by taking her father's hand, and Mary prayed. "Father, we thank you for the food we have when others don't have any breakfast this morning. Please give us wisdom as we plan our day and give us your protection. Amen."

"Amen," Lizzy repeated with her father.

She scooped grits onto her spoon, but before she could put it into her mouth, a knock on the back door froze her midmotion.

All three turned toward the garage.

Who would visit at this hour of the morning?

Dad rose and signaled for them to remain seated. "Stay quiet."

She grabbed Mary's hand and squeezed it, receiving reassuring pressure.

She hadn't realized she'd been holding her breath until Dad's voice allowed her to take in air.

"Rebecca," Dad said in the mudroom. "What a relief to see you."

Mary jumped off her stool, knocking it over in her haste to see her mother.

Lizzy followed as Mary plowed into her mother's arms.

A giant group hug formed.

"Can I get in on that hug?"

A large man, at least six and a half feet tall, though trim and muscular, opened his arms, blue eyes sparkling above a bushy-gray beard.

"I'm so sorry." Aunt Rebecca moved away from the group and hooked her arm with the giant's. "This is Al Carhart. He traveled with me and the other missionaries who evacuated Honduras."

"We're grateful to you for getting Rebecca to us safely, Al." Dad clapped the other man on the shoulder and shook his hand. "You're welcome to stay with us. It's not safe in this city right now."

"You'd be surprised." Al pumped Dad's hand. "We've seen worse on our way here. But the cities are more dangerous than the countryside, by far."

Al smiled at Mary. "By those gentle hazel eyes, I can tell you must be Mary. Your mom has told me a lot about you on our trip here."

"Are you hungry? We were just sitting down for breakfast," Dad said.

"No, but thanks." The giant held up a hand. "We're good."

"Then let's settle you in the living room." Dad led the way. "You can leave your bags in the mudroom for now."

Breakfast forgotten, Mary snuggled into her mother's arms on the couch, her eyes red with occasional escapee tears she swiped at. "Tell us what it's like out there. How's everyone back at the mission?"

"It's not good, honey." Aunt Rebecca stole a glance at Al, who shrugged. "It hit the Honduran people just as hard as those here in the United States. I can't believe how fast we lost so many."

Aunt Rebecca's sandy brown hair slithered over her shoulder as she craned around her daughter to meet Lizzy's eyes. "I'm so sorry about your mom, Lizzy. You must miss her terribly."

The reminder hit like a gut punch. Tears burned her eyes, and she mopped them with her sleeve. How could she have more to shed? There should be some sort of limit.

She couldn't make eye contact. So, head ducked, she whispered, "Thank you."

Al broke the ensuing silence. "I've got family here in the States as well. Up in Atlanta—two boys. Both are married, no grandkids yet, but that's where I'm heading next." He spread his hands. "I'm journeying back to Honduras once I've made sure they're safe. They'll need me even more now that they're short-staffed."

Aunt Rebecca nodded, then focused on Mary with a squeeze, tipping their foreheads together, their Tilbrook noses in matching profile. "What do you think? You ready to head back to help? It's going to be harder than before."

Without a moment's pause or an apparent second thought, Mary nodded. "Of course."

Dad's face was tough to read, but his jaw hardened as if he'd made some decision. "I agree. We need to move out of the city.

But Honduras? That doesn't seem like a wise choice. You won't have anything to bring to the people there. The churches won't send much to other countries when we're struggling at home."

"We still have hope," Aunt Rebecca said. "That's what we'll bring."

Dad shook his head. "Hope can be a dangerous commodity sometimes."

"And it can be worth more than gold as well," she said.

«»

Aunt Rebecca prepared dinner that night. They all sat at the dining room table as she brought out a steaming casserole dish. The smell of fish and cheese combined was suspicious—an odd assault on Lizzy's nose.

"What are we having?" she asked. "It looks like noodles, but I don't recognize the smell."

Aunt Rebecca winked. "It's tuna surprise."

That didn't help. Lizzy's nose scrunched. "What's the surprise?"

With a laugh, Aunt Rebecca sat in Mom's chair. "You'll be surprised how edible it is. I made a casserole base of macaroni and cheese from a box with no milk and no butter."

Lizzy smiled back. It was good to have something to be positive about, if even for a moment.

Aunt Rebecca grasped Mary's hand and started the chain-reaction circle of hand holding. Then looked to Dad. "Dan, would you like to ask for the blessing?"

Wiggling in her seat, Lizzy struggled not to gape. She hadn't heard her father pray in years. Sometimes she'd see him mouthing words, but since Mom frowned on religion, he kept his thoughts to himself. Why did he always have to be the peacemaker?

Now he bowed his head and spoke aloud. "Father, thank you for bringing my sister back to us. Please keep us all safe, no matter where we end up going. And thank you for the culinary treat we're about to enjoy. May the surprise be a pleasant one. Amen."

She giggled with her own chorused amen.

They passed their dishes to Aunt Rebecca to serve as the casserole dish was too hot to hand around. When her aunt passed her plate back, the food looked mushy, but knowing what it was, Lizzy had grown accustomed to the smell.

She lifted her fork and tested a tentative bite. Yup. Macaroni and cheese with tuna and maybe some sort of condensed soup mixed in. Probably mushroom, if the bits of brown were any indicator. "Not bad."

Her aunt smiled before she took a bite.

They were eating and plotting solutions to their problems. It appeared Dad wanted to emphasize all the potential problems associated with a trip back to Honduras.

The explosion of gunshots cut the argument short. Distant screams followed.

Al jumped up from his chair and motioned to Aunt Rebecca, Mary, and Lizzy. "Move into the kitchen. Stay down and away from the windows."

She heard Dad and Al's shuffling footfalls to the front windows, then silence.

Her heart raced. What was going on?

Aunt Rebecca motioned for Mary and her to stay put, but just as she started to move out of the kitchen toward the foyer, Dad and Al soundlessly joined them in the kitchen.

"I've got an RV," Dad addressed Al. "It's stocked and ready to go. Extra gas as well."

With a nod, Al rubbed his hands together. "Since they're looting the home down the street, we need to get out of here."

She wanted to vomit. Looting? In Columbus, Georgia? And here in their neighborhood. An area full of business professionals, not hoodlums.

"Where will we go?" If this part of town wasn't safe, where would be?

"Diane's place." Dad clamped a hand on Al's shoulder. "She's my wife's best friend and mentor. They live in a gated community. It's farther north—secluded. They've got plenty there. I'm sure of it."

When Al's face registered hesitance, she chimed in. "Dad's right—it'll be safe there."

Dad patted Mary's arm. "Get your duffle bag. Pack as much as you can into it, but only necessities. Sturdy clothes for hiking. Leave room to pack canned and boxed food from the pantry."

He pointed to Lizzy next. "You too. Only what's necessary and leave as much room for food as you can. Be quick, though. The looters won't take long to get to this house."

Lizzy sprinted back to her bedroom as they scattered to their individual rooms. What was important? A frantic buzz ran down her spine, then settled in her chest. She needed to calm down, or she'd never be able to think.

First things first. She dashed to the closet and dragged out her backpack and small suitcase. After flinging them onto the bed, she opened each, then tossed out her school notebooks from the book bag. Who cared about school assignments when mobs were raging on the streets?

Next, she hurried to the dresser, tore open the top drawer, and grabbed socks and underwear, then down to the next drawers for shirts, pajamas, shorts, and leggings. No time to pick out favorites or best fitting. She threw them into the suitcase and darted to the closet.

Precious moments wasted away as she searched through the flimsy heels and sandals for her hiking boots. After she found them, she pulled jeans and gym shoes out and pushed them into the suitcase.

It wouldn't shut. There was too much. What to leave behind? Her mind kept circling back to the popping sounds on the street. She couldn't think.

Grabbing handfuls of clothing, she jammed it into the book bag and stuffed with all her might. Wait—she was supposed to leave room for food. Now what?

She sat on her suitcase and forced the zipper shut. Or at least almost shut. Close enough.

Dad's head popped in through the doorway. His voice was stern. "Let's go, kiddo. We need to get out of here."

She glanced around the room, frantic not to forget anything important. The phone in her pocket contained every photo of Mom she'd ever taken, but she wanted something else.

"Take my bags," she yelled at Dad. "I need to grab one more thing of Mom's."

"We don't have time, Lizzy."

Dad snatched the backpack and threw the strap over his shoulder, then snagged the suitcase off the bed. He put his hand out to grasp her by the wrist, but she twisted away and ran out of the room.

As fast as her feet would allow, she sprinted across the game room, through the dining room, cut through the corner of the kitchen, then the great room, ending in her parents' bedroom. She targeted the closet and flung clothes out of her way as she burrowed in.

There had to be something, anything. Then she found it—her mother's high school jacket. Mom had been a cheerleader—one of the cool kids in her day. She'd had pictures of herself and her friends in the photo albums she dragged out now and then. This jacket was in several photos. Mom liked to brag that the jacket still fit after all these years.

Lizzy wrapped her arms around the coat and inhaled. It smelled of her mother's perfume. This would do.

"Lizzy," Dad hollered from the mudroom. "Now!"

With one more glance around the room that had been her mother's refuge, she followed her father's voice to join him, and they rushed out of their home—a haven that was no longer secure—into the uncertainty before them.

Chapter Eleven

Lizzy shadowed her father, sprinting out of the house and into the carport. With the entire family gathered around the car, the truck, and all their luggage, it was a tight fit.

Outside the enclosed area, their RV waited underneath a shelter yards away. The smell of smoke sent her eyes searching further out. Black clouds rolled into the air a few blocks over.

"I parked on the other side of the house, but we were close to empty when we got here," Al said to Dad. "Not sure how far my car will get us."

"The truck's fueled. Follow close once we're out of the driveway." Dad tossed the keys to Al.

They slammed luggage and duffels into the back of the truck. Then Al, Aunt Rebecca, and Mary scrambled into the cab.

Lizzy raced to the RV behind her father, with her mother's jacket clutched under her arm. The moment the locks popped, she hopped into the vehicle.

"Buckle in." Dad tossed the suitcases behind the driver's seat. "We're about to find out how much speed a recreational vehicle can manage."

A gunshot exploded, sending shocks shivering up her spine. That was close. Too close.

"Keep your head down." He pushed her lower into the seat.

Screeching tires on the cement drew her attention to the side mirror. Dad's truck bounced out of the carport and spun to face the road, ready to follow them.

Wow. Dad sure managed to start the vehicle, perform a wild three-point turn, and speed down the short drive to the road—fast. She'd have sworn he never even looked before exiting the driveway onto the road.

They zoomed through their subdivision, the surrounding scenes etching into her memory.

Armed men, brandishing weapons like some sort of war movie, crawled the neighborhood. One of her favorite houses on the block flamed red and orange near the roofline, while a strange man rummaged through the car in the driveway. A group of men kicked in a door of a home near the subdivision's entrance. As the entryway opened, they rushed in with whoops and hollers.

Please, let no one be home today.

Inertia forced her body backward in her seat when Dad stomped on the gas pedal. Preoccupied with what was going on in the homes they passed, she hadn't noticed the throng wandering around the entrance to their neighborhood.

"Hold on." Dad continued speeding up. "We're not stopping for anyone or anything."

A glance in the side mirror showed their truck practically glued to the camper's rear bumper. If Dad hit the brakes, the truck would be a permanent fixture in the back of the RV.

Lizzy held her breath and stayed low. The mob had noted

them and held their positions, brandishing weapons.

"Ahh!" Dad screamed, his eyes fierce and determined in a way she'd never experienced before.

One hand swiped sideways through the air. "Move!"

The RV swayed back and forth. She had no idea how they passed through the multitude of people without plowing someone over—but they did. In her rearview, a large rock ricocheted off the truck, but Al didn't slow.

Never had she been so grateful they lived on the outskirts of town. She couldn't imagine what it would be like to go through more of these zones of discontent.

They passed through smatterings of activity. People wandered the streets with guns. Others packed vehicles, hoping to escape. Soon they exited the residential area and rode on a two lane. Pine trees flew past on both sides.

"You all right?" Dad held his hand out.

She couldn't tell who shook the hardest when she grasped his fingers.

"I'm good." Her escaping laugh sounded more maniacal than humorous. His appearance worried her. "Your face is pretty red. Maybe we need to pull over and let you calm down."

His return laugh quavered. "We're not stopping until we get to Diane's subdivision."

A glimpse in the rearview mirror revealed the truck was still on their tail.

"What if Diane isn't at home?" Though that was a possibility, it wasn't the question weighing on her. "We can't get in unless she buzzes us in."

"I'm sure they're home."

Mom's goal had been to get to the C-Suite level at her company, then move into Diane's subdivision. The address was a status symbol. She'd targeted a move within a few short years. If she'd landed more clients, they'd have packed up and moved.

Columbus, Georgia, was a simple town to get around. They told new residents you could reach anything you needed within a fifteen-minute drive. In roughly that time, they pulled up to a gate protecting the high-end area Diane called home.

The speaker box had a scanner to swipe a fob for residents and a keypad for a code for close family and friends. An intercom to contact a household was also on the pole if you didn't qualify for either of the first two options.

Though Mom had always called Diane her mentor, she'd rarely visited at her private residence. What did that say about their relationship? Was Diane just a resource for Mom to get to the top?

Or perhaps it was the opposite. Mom was a means for Diane's career growth.

Either way, Lizzy's nerves jangled as Dad pushed the intercom for Diane's home. What if they weren't welcome?

The box crackled, and a female voice came out. "Yes?"

Dad leaned out of the RV window as far as he could and announced himself. "Diane, it's Daniel Tilbrook, Jennifer's husband."

The silence stretched out too long.

"Hello?" His confident voice wavered. "Diane? Did you hear me?"

The camera above the gate moved higher, most likely taking in the view behind their RV to the truck following them.

More static erupted from the box, a male voice this time. "What do you want?"

Dad forced a smile toward the camera, then spoke to the box.

"Our neighborhood isn't safe right now. I've got Lizzy with me, as well as my sister, niece, and a friend. We're hoping to join up with you for the night. Get our bearings, so to speak."

He waved at the watching eye.

"Sorry, we don't have the room." The man didn't sound the least bit apologetic. "You need to move on. You're blocking the gate."

Dad's eyebrows furrowed. "Is Diane there? Does she know it's Dan Tilbrook? Jen's husband?"

"Move on. Or I'll call the police."

That was it—denied. No friends in that home.

"What are we going to do?" Lizzy cringed at her whine. Panic rose to choke her. "Do you have any other friends?"

Dad shook his head. "They all live on the south side of town. It's not safe to drive that direction."

She knew the truth of the statement before he'd said the words. While Mom sought resources, Dad gravitated toward those who needed a friend. Most of those friends lived in poorer communities. If looting had arrived at the north end, no way was the south side safe.

With a click of his seatbelt, he opened his door and climbed out. He shut the door, then leaned in the open window. "Wait here. I'm going to talk to your aunt and Al."

The pounding in her chest had to be audible. She pivoted in her seat to keep focus on her father's retreating form. What if looters trailed them, soon to catch up? If he didn't get back in the RV, she'd join him at the other vehicle. She hated to be alone.

"Ahh!" She jumped when a squirrel hopped off the gate and onto the windshield. It sprang again, onto the RV roof. Her scream must have scared the animal as much as it had frightened her.

She clamped a hand over her mouth, closed her eyes, and took a deep breath.

In—one, two, three. Out—one, two, three.

If she didn't get her heart rate under control, she'd need a paper bag next.

The driver's door opened, and she started again.

"It's me." Dad took his seat and buckled in. He put his hand on hers. "We're fine. We've got a plan."

All she could manage was a nod. A tear slipped down her cheek, and she let it fall.

Her brain buzzed, unable to think. No home—no friends.

"Callaway Gardens has plenty of secluded places we can camp for the night. We'll get our bearings and figure out where we're headed."

He patted her hand, then put the RV into reverse.

Thoughts of beautiful flowers, expansive walking paths, and bike trails soothed her. She'd played on those beaches when she was little. Yes, that would be a perfect spot to camp for the night. She grasped onto the life raft the idea provided.

Within an hour, they arrived at the gardens. Since many others had beaten them to the destination, vehicles lined the various fields and pathways with tents and RVs of all sizes.

One family set up camp in their truck bed. A twin mattress with cartoon character sheets peeked out from under a tented blanket. Tiny eyes peered from an opening, a curious look on a boy's small face. A man with a sidearm leaned against the open tailgate, staring at the newcomers.

They reached the end of the long line of campers and pulled in. Dad put the vehicle in park and let out a huge breath. "Here we are. You, okay?"

What to say in response? She didn't know.

No. She did know.

She wasn't okay. Nothing was right.

The worry oozing from every wrinkle lining her father's eyes convinced her to keep herself in check. "I'm fine. What do we do next?"

Blue eyes focused ahead, narrowing above the Tilbrook nose. He twisted his grip on the steering wheel. Was he expecting some deep revelation to come from it?

She tried to think of something supportive and pithy to break the tension. Nothing came to mind.

Both started at a knock on the driver's side window.

A grimace tightened Al's face. He motioned to Dad to join him outside the RV. Dad opened the door but paused before exiting. "Why don't you see about getting a campground set up for tonight?"

She nodded. Maybe the fear in her belly would ease soon.

After he'd left the vehicle, she sat frozen in place, unsure what setting up camp involved. The storage compartments held sleeping bags. Mom had gone all-out, shopping for accessories to stock the camper before giving it to Dad. For once, Lizzy was certain Dad would be grateful for her mother's excesses.

While Lizzy pondered what to do next, Mary walked up to the passenger door and motioned for her to put the window down.

"Now that was one scary ride." Tucking wisps of sandy hair behind her ear, Mary jittered from foot to foot once the window was open. "Did you see the mob breaking down that door?"

"Most frightening thing I've ever seen." Lizzy opened her door and wobbled to the ground. "I can't believe what's happening."

"Your dad said you were going to work on getting the RV set up for tonight—said I should help."

Various campers huddled around cook fires, recreational vehicles, trucks, and automobiles. People had taken off with whatever they could manage in a short time.

One family had a microwave oven in the back of their trunk and a small generator they were trying to get started. She wouldn't have thought to try that.

But she had her own setup to do. Mary had been roughing it for years at the mission. Maybe she'd be a better resource than watching the other people. "Have you ever camped before? I only know what I've seen in movies and the brochure Mom showed me before she bought this thing." She hooked a thumb back toward the camper.

The laugh that escaped her cousin's lips seemed anything but comical. "Well, coz, let me tell you." Mary knocked on the RV's side door. "If the poor folks around our mission had one of these to live in, they'd be singing praises in the chapel night and day."

Ouch. Cringing, Lizzy wanted to smack herself on the forehead. Mary was right. They had more than a lot of the other people in her view had.

Pull yourself together, Lizzy Tilbrook!

She opened the door to the camper's living area and a set of steps slid out, inviting them inside. "Let's check it out."

They stepped into a living room-dining-room-kitchen combination with a couch, table, and a bunk bed over the driver's cab. Creature comforts packed the tiny space. At the touch of a button, the slide out crept away from the center, creating a larger living area. Though she'd never been in a tight space that held so much, the area's efficiency was obvious.

A small refrigerator held canned soda and bottled water already cooling. Opening various doors and drawers revealed pots, pans, dishes, silverware, a can opener, and other utensils.

Opposite the kitchen, a miniature bathroom nestled behind a door. No way could two people be in the bathroom simultaneously, but all the essentials were there.

A sliding door at the vehicle's far end opened to a bedroom with a queen-sized bed snuggled between two nightstands.

This would be their new home. She peeked out a window at the neighboring truck bed with the mattress and blanket roof. Guilt overwhelmed her. She'd been afforded luxurious accommodation. With nothing to complain about, she would do what she could to help others.

12

Chapter Twelve

ire. Something was on fire! Lizzy shot up out of bed, panic rising in her throat. The unfamiliar surroundings confused her. "Dad!"

A body sprang up next to her in the bed.

She yelped and clutched the covers tight to her chest.

Mary's wide eyes blinked back at her. "What's wrong?"

"Sorry." Lizzy closed her eyes and tried to slow her breathing. "I was just confused there for a second."

The previous evening, they'd staked out the various territories in the camper. Aunt Rebecca was in the loft above the driver's cabin. Al slept on the dining table that lowered to the bench seats and converted to a bed. Dad claimed the couch. Mary and Lizzy shared the master bedroom.

The smoke came from campfires. Other campers preparing their breakfasts.

She couldn't have slept even a few hours last night. When sleep came, she dreamed she was back in school. Mom was alive and at work. Everything was back to normal—a dream, a pipe dream.

Reality was nowhere near the realm of normal.

"Well, we're awake now." Mary pushed the covers off. "Might as well get breakfast started."

The thought brought her hollow stomach to mind. Lizzy barely choked down a few dry crackers last night. By the time they'd gotten everything set up, no one was hungry enough to attempt cooking, but they'd have to figure it out, eventually.

"I saw grits in the pantry last night." She pushed the covers off and crawled to the end of the bed to get out. "Tight quarters."

She'd better get used to small living spaces occupied by multiple people. Either that or turn into an outdoor lover. With five people sharing one RV, it was going to be squishy.

Mary beat her to the bathroom. But they'd slept in their clothes, so she didn't need to get dressed. Bathroom time would have to be scheduled too. Living this way was going to be a challenge.

«»

"Anyone want to go for a walk?" Lizzy asked after the cleanup. "I don't think I can stay in this confinement much longer."

She'd never thought of herself as claustrophobic until they'd all been inside the compartment cooking, eating, and now cleaning up. If she bumped into Mary one more time, she'd say something rather impolite. She was sure of it.

"I don't think we should wander around." Dad put the last spoon into the silverware drawer. "Things were quiet last night, but we're better off plotting our next destination."

"Rebecca and I discussed our plans last night." Al nodded toward her aunt. "We'd like to borrow the truck. I need to see my sons in Atlanta. Then we'll head toward our mission headquarters. It's time we got reconnected and back to work."

Lizzy rubbed her thrumming temples. Seriously, who could

believe their dedication? The world was falling apart, and they couldn't care less. They only wanted to help others.

Her father nodded. "I figured you'd be on your way soon. It's not like we're going to need the truck. It's too big for us to pull with the RV. Keep it. I just hope you can find fuel."

Aunt Rebecca walked the few steps to her brother and hugged him. "Thanks, Dan. I knew we could count on you." She stepped back from the embrace and looked between him and Lizzy. "But what are you two going to do? You're welcome to come with us, of course, but it won't be easy."

Shaking his head, Dad pulled Lizzy to his side. "We're not cut out for that type of work, no matter how much I admire you folks for doing it." He rubbed her arm as if to warm her. "No, we're going to head away from the cities, at least as far as we can—see if we can find some open land. I always wanted to try my hand at self-sufficiency. This is my chance."

Self-sufficiency? What did that even mean? Going to Honduras with Aunt Rebecca and Mary would be terrifying, but the ambiguity of leaving everything she'd ever known was no less frightening.

A tap on the screen door disrupted the conversation.

"Hello? Lizzy… Mary… are you guys here?"

The voice seemed familiar, but she couldn't place it. Mary reached the door first and screeched. "Harper!"

Harper? How could that be? What were the chances?

With a yank of the door, Mary jumped out of the camper and wrapped Harper in a hug. They danced a mini jig of reunion.

Between squeals, Harper said, "I thought that was your truck. I can't believe I found you."

Dad nudged Lizzy toward the celebration. "Go on. You don't know how many chances you'll get to see your school friends again."

Friends? That was the last word she'd use to describe her relationship with Harper, and the girls couldn't want her with them. Dad didn't have a clue about the drama. He was so oblivious sometimes.

So Lizzy walked toward the doorway as if headed for a firing squad. Waving, Dad urged her to join the girls outside. Perhaps if she went out and skirted around them, they'd never notice. She could flee to the cab or the truck until the meeting ended.

As she stepped out the door, Mary was telling the story of their escape from the city. Lizzy tucked her chin and headed toward the RV cab, hopeful they'd ignore her.

No such luck.

"Lizzy." Mary reached out a hand and waggled her fingers. "Come on and tell Harper what you saw yesterday."

Lizzy froze on the spot. If she faced the girls, she'd have no option but to talk to Harper and deal with whatever anger remained over her deception.

If she just kept walking, though, she'd be running away from the problem for the rest of her life—might as well take her lumps now.

"You've covered most of it already." She joined the pair. "It was a wild ride."

Moments ago, Harper had been frantic with excitement. Now, she gave Lizzy a cool look and slid her hands into her jeans pockets. "Good morning, Lizzy. I'm glad to see you and Mary are both safe."

The greeting couldn't have been more stilted if Harper had been the queen of England.

Lizzy's spine stiffened under the other girl's scrutiny. "Thanks. Glad you made it out too."

Mary looked back and forth between them as if watching an imaginary ping-pong ball being volleyed. The silence continued until Mary planted her hands on her hips and huffed out a breath.

"Well, no sense in ignoring the elephant in the yard, is there?" Mary moved to the folding lawn chairs they'd set up the night before. "Let's sit and chat for a bit, shall we?"

Great. Now a quick getaway was out of the question.

Lizzy's heart pounded over the confrontation ahead. Why had she gone along with Mom's plan in the first place?

They sat after Mary arranged the chairs in a circle so they faced each other.

Lizzy rested with her hands under her thighs, unable to find anything better to do with them. With them under her legs, no one could see them tremble. If she didn't get past this soon, her breakfast would be on its way back up.

"The world changed." Mary started the conversation. "We need each other now more than ever. Some things are better off left in the past."

Lizzy plucked up every ounce of courage she owned—and borrowed some from the future as well. Then she looked right at Harper. Whew. At least, she was still staring at the ground. Perhaps the other girl was as uncomfortable with the conversation as Lizzy was.

"Harper," Lizzy said.

Harper's head shot up, and she met Lizzy's gaze with her own.

"I'm sorry," she continued. "I should never have set you up the way I did. It was wrong."

Mary nodded and sat forward on her chair as if anticipating a tense movie scene.

Harper did the opposite by turning her gaze back to her sneakers.

The two moves combined to bolster Lizzy's resolve. "I've never had real friends before. But I'm sure friends don't throw each other under the bus over stupid things like the class president's role."

Though she didn't make eye contact, Harper looked back up and smiled. "None of my friends would have. I thought you were one of them, though."

Now *she* had to break off eye contact and look at the grass. It needed to be mowed. But that was a thought for another time. *Focus, Lizzy.*

"I should have been." Something damp slid down her cheek.

How could she be crying over this? She hadn't even liked Harper.

But she knew why—truly. Because she'd always used people instead of learning about them and knowing them, she'd kept them at bay. Allowed no one into her life close enough to hurt her. Just like Mom.

Look how that ended. Mom died, and no one was there to mourn her besides Lizzy and Dad. She didn't want that for her own life—she wanted real friends like Mary had.

Another set of sneakers appeared in her field of vision, next to her own. A hand touched her shoulder, and when she looked up, Harper bent down and wrapped her arms around Lizzy.

So, this was a friend's hug. It felt wonderful and brought fresh tears to her eyes.

She stood and accepted the embrace as the peace offering she needed.

"Yay!" Mary whooped out, then jumped out of her chair, and joined them in a group squeeze.

They all began laughing, then crying, then snorted at their tears.

Once they'd gotten past the worst of the sniffles, Harper made eye contact again.

"I forgive you." She winked at Lizzy. "But don't do that again. Friends?"

"Friends," she said.

She was going to enjoy having friends in her life.

«»

That evening, Lizzy joined the family around the fire pit. They'd found a bag of marshmallows tucked away in the pantry and roasted them on sticks over flames. She loved watching the puffy white cylinders turn brown, and then sizzle. The smoke from them sweet in her nose.

No blackened treats for her. The edges needed to crisp to a golden brown before she devoured the outer layer, then sent the softened inside back to the flames.

Beside her, Al's stick came out of the blaze with a flaming glob on the end. He blew to extinguish the treat.

"Finally got in touch with my boys when the phones were up last night. They're fine. In fact, we're going to head out in the morning to meet up with them," he told Dad. "No sense waiting any longer. I don't see anything getting better soon, and people need help now more than ever."

Dad placed two fresh marshmallows on his stick and poked them into the fire. "Lizzy and I will stick around this area. There must be other campgrounds or places to park." He pulled the flaming orbs back out and doused them with a quick puff of air. "I've always wanted to try my hand at farming. Living off the land, as they say. And if we stay close by, our gas will last longer."

Other campfires dotted the fields and forest. Fireflies lit all around them. Somewhere in the dark, a child laughed against the backdrop of murmured conversations. It was a beautiful night.

Plucking the crispy skin off her marshmallow, she popped it into her mouth and savored the sweet crunch.

A distant scream splintered their peaceful cocoon. Her heart hammering, she jumped up and scanned the darkness. Gunshots followed more screams.

"Scratch those morning plans." Al threw his stick into the fire pit. "We're leaving now."

"Agreed," Dad said. "Let's get out of here."

The speed with which they packed the lawn chairs, barbeque utensils, and laundry hung to dry would've beaten any records in existence. It wasn't so much packing—more like throwing everything into the vehicles in piles.

It took only minutes, and who knew if they'd missed something in the dark. But the sounds drew closer by the second. Headlights headed their way.

Mary grabbed her in a hug. "I'm going to miss you and Uncle Dan."

Hot tears slid down Lizzy's cheeks as she returned the embrace. It was unfair to lose her cousin, who'd taught her so much in such a short time. Just when she'd decided she wanted friends, she was losing the best one she'd ever had.

"Be safe," she said. "I'll text you whenever I get enough signal or until my phone dies."

"Lizzy, Mary, we gotta go." Dad hollered from the RV cab. "Now!"

Mary ran to the truck where Aunt Rebecca and Al waited. With a last wave, she got in the back of the cab, and they sped off, kicking up grass with their departure.

"Lizzy!"

She sprinted to join her father. The screams and gunshots drew closer.

The moment she sat in the cab, Dad stomped the gas pedal. Her door slammed shut with the forward momentum, and her body pressed into her seat.

As they sped away from the crowds, they joined uneven lines of vehicles making their own quick exits. Dad bobbed and weaved as best he could in the clumsy vehicle, getting way too close to the ditches. He used the berm to get around slower-moving vehicles.

A dodge or two later, they were out of the tangle and onto a dirt road. Only then did he slow, and she realized the maddening ding in her head was the seat belt warning.

She pulled the restraint around herself and clicked it. Dad followed suit, which ended the warning, and the cab silenced.

Though he slowed the vehicle to a reasonable pace for a dirt road, he didn't stop. They drove in silence away from the mayhem, searching for a new home.

13

Chapter Thirteen

wo years later...

Lizzy didn't bother opening her eyes. It was morning, but she ached to stay in bed. A new day and a new camping location.

She stretched her sore arms and hit the ceiling. How she missed morning stretches in her old bed. She'd avoided sleeping in the loft over the driver's cabin for as long as she could. The couch had grown lumpier by the day until she'd been forced to try the smaller space.

The narrow opening felt like dozing in a coffin.

"Morning, sunshine," Dad said. "We'll need to scout for firewood before I can cobble up breakfast."

More work. She'd done more physical labor in the last two years than she'd done in her entire life before the collapse. They'd done everything they could to economize and make their resources last. That meant cooking over a fire when they could find wood. Hunting up propane was hard these days, and their previous fill-up might be their last.

Everything they consumed had the potential to be their last.

They'd moved around from place to place, finding work here and there, scrounging up food where they could.

As time wore on, life changed little by little until her old life was a fond memory. If she'd known what it would be like to live hand-to-mouth, she'd have eaten more ice cream, luxuriated in hot showers with shampoo, and savored macaroni and cheese, even if it wasn't the blue box.

She would have cherished every minute with Mom.

Why hadn't she understood friendships better when she had the chance to make some?

Sliding from underneath the covers, she climbed down the ladder to the RV's floor. Her socks lay on the couch where she'd left them the night before. A new hole opened up in the sole of the left one. If only she'd grabbed more socks the night they'd taken off. Who knew how hard they'd be to come by? If only she'd taken that Family and Consumer Sciences class and figured out how to sew and repair clothing.

"You know what day is coming up next week?" She looked at her father for signs of recognition, wondering if he'd remember.

A sad smile greeted her when he made eye contact. "Yes, of course. Mom died two years ago come Tuesday."

How could it only have been two years ago? An eternity had passed since they'd all been together in their family home.

Last year, they'd returned to her grave site, then back to their home. She wished they'd skipped the trip to the house. Its devastated state stole her beautiful memories.

The door was wide open as if they'd just forgotten to close it behind them one day. When they crossed the threshold, though, the destruction horrified her. Everything of value was gone.

Someone had even yanked out the toilet.

Who does that?

"Are we going back to visit her grave?"

"I'm sorry." Dad joined her on the couch. He put his arm around her and snugged her to his side with his best daddy hug. "We don't have enough gas. Even if we did, Columbus isn't safe to visit. Unless we can walk someplace to work for some fuel, we're going to be stuck here for a while."

Though true, hearing the words made her cringe. She didn't like to think of her mother being there by herself, but then, it wasn't really Mom in that grave. Mom was gone.

Sighing, she wiggled her socks onto her feet.

No sense focusing on the negatives. They'd both agreed to concentrate on the positive aspects of their new life. It was now their grand adventure—or at least that was their theme for what they had left.

They'd pulled into the driveway in the dark last night, so they weren't sure what resources they'd find. The home on the property looked deserted. A quick knock on the door and walk around the house confirmed no occupants the previous evening.

Picking up her shoes, she stuffed her feet in them and stood. She flashed the happiest grin she could manage. "Ready to explore our new place?"

He returned the smile, opened the door, and gave a grand wave toward the outdoors. "After you, my dear."

They'd stopped in so many locations over the past two years. One trip back to Columbus cured them of the desire to stay in the crowded and violent area. The fewer people around, the safer they were. They didn't stay in any place for long. No place felt like home, so they continued to search.

The muggy morning air dampened her skin. It would be another hot day in the South. The morning light revealed a small farm.

"Let's take a walk, shall we?" Dad closed the door behind them and started toward the ranch house they'd parked in front of. "Perhaps the folks who own this place left some clues behind about when they'll be back."

A swing dangled over the porch, and she could picture herself on a lazy, hot day, swinging and drinking sweet tea. Someday. She missed lazy days. If she were lucky, perhaps she could even have a girlfriend to share secrets with. Mary, Ava, and Harper invaded her mental wanderings.

Would she ever see them again?

As they walked past the porch, she eyed the welcome mat. Boswell arched over a wreath of daisies stamped on it. So that's who lived here before. The Boswells. Had any teens lived in the household?

Continuing around the house, they wandered into the backyard. It nestled beside an expanse of neglected fields.

"This used to be a cattle ranch," Dad said in a wistful tone. "What I wouldn't give to make this a working farm again. Then we'd live well."

She understood. "I'd love to stop moving around so much. It'd be nice to wake up in the same place every morning, like we did in the old days."

They reached the fence separating the overgrown backyard and the grassy pasture.

Dad leaned against the post and placed a finger on the wire connecting the columns. "Electricity's off in the fence. Most likely the power is out for the entire farm, but it's possible there's a break in the wire someplace."

They'd spent a month working for a cattle rancher last year, so Dad knew a thing or two about fences and cattle. What she knew wouldn't fill a thimble, but she remembered how cute the calves were. The faraway look in his eyes said he was thinking back to the other ranch.

"I still feel bad we had to leave that farm." She threaded her arm through his. "If I'd been able to do more, they might not have kicked us out."

He nudged her. "Wasn't your fault, kiddo. I'm glad we got out of there, anyway. Mrs. Johnson saved us more trouble than not. Her husband watched you too close for my comfort."

The dirty old man ogled her one too many times in his wife's presence.

She shuddered over the morning the farmer's wife kicked them to the curb.

"You take your hussy of a child and get on down the road. We don't need your help any longer," she'd said.

Jobs were hard to find these days, so it hurt to lose one her father enjoyed so much.

They spent the rest of the morning investigating the property. A creek flowed from a natural spring, and the water tasted clean, which was a tremendous bonus. Watercress grew along the edge.

That evening, they sat by a fire pit they'd dug and surrounded with rocks. There were no fire companies anymore, so they did all they could to prevent wildfires. Not too long ago they'd raced to flee a campground in Pine Mountain and just missed being consumed in the flames.

A rabbit roasted on a spit in front of them. With this their last bit of meat, the snares they'd set today better capture more critters soon. But for now, she'd be grateful for what they had.

"Do you think we can make this place work, Dad?"

They'd passed through a village on their way to the farm.

Though the people stared at the newcomers, they seemed like hardworking people, not marauders who lived by stealing from others. It looked like a place she could call home.

"I'd sure love to try." He pulled a leg off the rabbit. "Looks like supper is ready."

They divided the meat between them, then bowed their heads.

"Father, thank you for bringing us here to rest." Dad prayed for them. "Please help us find a way to stay here and feed ourselves. Thank you for tonight's food. Amen."

"Amen," she said.

The words reminded her of her cousin, and she hoped Mary was doing well and had all she needed tonight.

As for herself, she dreamed of having a friend, now that she understood what friendship was all about. Somehow, it felt different on this farm. Like they were meant to be here. They'd have to trust God brought them here for a purpose.

Time would tell.

THE BEGINNING...

***Take a sneak peek
at the next installment!***
Collapse: The Death of Friendship

Collapse Book One: The Death of Friendship ~ Chapter One

The framed painting oozed peace and tranquility. If Jan Worthington could have crawled into the canvas to become a part of the landscape, she would have. Lush green fields where tall grasses waved in the gentle breeze were the center of the piece, but the eye-catcher was the girl on a swing underneath an oak in the painting's corner. Her wide-brimmed purple hat, Jan's favorite color, rippled back with the motion, and with the way her feet flew up into the air, life must be carefree for this child.

Jan reached to touch the picture, wanting it, but even more so, wanting to sit on such a swing in such a place, not a care in the world to pull her back down to earth. This was how her life should have been. But at sixteen, she knew a different life. One that wasn't untroubled or without worry.

The artist in her ached to explore the textures of the paint's ridges. The painter perfectly captured the wind's movement and the swing's momentum with their brushstrokes. She longed to hold a paintbrush again and stroke the canvas with colors and textures.

That wasn't her life anymore though. Chicken coop cleaning, calf wrangling, and not nearly enough parties now overtook her days. She should be cheering the football team to a win this weekend, not searching for food alternatives to replace everything they'd lost.

An elbow to her ribs jerked her out of the picturesque places her mind had gone to. "Hello. Earth to Jan, where are you, Jan?"

Her BFF and next-door neighbor, Renee Boswell, was a great cheer buddy but had no eye for art. With her golden blond hair under a ball cap and her dark suntanned arms and face, she looked anything but her German-American heritage.

Chin high, Jan swiped at the red hair poking out of a similar baseball cap, then jammed her hands on her slim hips, her fingers grazing her best market-day jeans and T-shirt. "Can't you even take a minute to appreciate how much work went into this painting?"

"Yes, dear. It's a pretty picture." Renee turned from the painting and craned over the market tables spread along the huge field beside the auction barn. "But we've been standing here for like ten minutes already. The day's a'wastin.'"

Jan twitched her lips and let out a breath. "Fine." Turning to the vendor behind the table, she said, "It's an exquisite painting. I love your brushstrokes."

The white-haired man bowed his head in acknowledgment. "It's been a while since I had fresh materials. This was one of the last ones I created before Andy's Art Supply shut down. I hate to part with it, but if you can come up with a pound of that dried beef your mama makes, it's all yours."

An entire pound of dried beef? That wasn't going to happen. Practically a king's ransom these days. But the guy was so skinny, and the artwork was all he had to trade. One day, she would have all the art she wanted in her own place. One day.

She sniffed the air. Normally, the most prominent smell would be the auction barn. It took a lot to mask its stench, but something nearby smelled sweet. She grabbed her BFF's arm and tugged her toward the smell. "I smell sorghum."

They might be a little too old to be walking arm-in-arm through the market-day tables. But she didn't care. They had once been two of almost a dozen friends who had sleepovers and pillow fights. But most had to move away from Shiloh, Georgia, for their parents to find work.

"I think it's over this way." Renee hauled her down another line of tables, Jan's feet tripping along on the dirt path between the vendors.

Steam rose from an enormous cauldron over a fire. An elderly man stirred the contents with a wooden paddle, his thin gray hair frizzing in the steam. Pint-sized jars gleamed on the table to his right. The dark sorghum syrup would be a sweet addition to their pantry. Giant popcorn balls beckoned from a glass plate.

"Are you making molasses?" Jan asked.

"What do you think they're doing, goofball"—Renee elbowed her—"their laundry?"

As Jan giggled, the older woman at the table smiled. "Actually, the molasses is already in the container. We're turning it into taffy." She pointed at the row. "The smell always brings people in."

Candy was a rare treat. Since the variants started four years ago, Jan had fewer opportunities for the sweet things in life every year.

Closing her eyes, she breathed in deeply. Just standing here and indulging in smelling it was a treat. "I'm afraid to even ask how much the taffy costs."

The woman dabbed at her forehead, then tucked a handkerchief into her sleeve, and glanced over her shoulder at her husband. Absorbed in his task, he didn't look up.

"Tell you what…" Dropping her voice to a conspiratorial whisper, she winked. "I don't see too many young folks around here anymore. I'll trade you a full bag to share if you can get me a half-dozen jars of fruit. Deal?"

That would have been an excellent trade. But Mom was selling canned vegetables back at their table, not fruit. Mrs. Boswell, Renee's mom, was helping because they had nothing of their own to sell.

"Give us a little while." Her arm still linked through Renee's, Jan gave it a squeeze. "I've got a plan."

"What are you thinking?" Renee, always up for an adventure, asked as they ran together back to their table.

"I'll bet we can trade her some of Dad's dried beef and two jars of spinach."

Dried beef was a delicacy few could afford these days. Their expanding beef farm provided a few steers every year that Dad raised and butchered. Mom would salt and dry much of it for sale on market day.

Back at their table, Mom and Mrs. Boswell were busy with two different customers, negotiating a trade. Mom's thin arms shook as if she needed to sit down before exhaustion overtook her. Even with the white sun hat shading her face, sweat slicked along her hairline while her low-hanging ponytail snaked down the side of her neck onto her bright yellow "lucky" sales shirt.

As soon as Mom finished with her customer, Jan used her very best sad-puppy-dog look. That always worked on Mom. "Can we have a bag of dried beef and two jars of spinach?"

Mom shook her ponytail off her shoulder, the slippery dark strands complying. "What for?"

Jan pinched her BFF's arm to get her attention. This would

require a double team effort and help them continue to earn their nickname—Double Trouble.

"Candy?" Double down on the look and pull hands up into a pleading gesture.

When Renee joined in, eyes round and saddish, Mom laughed. "That's a steep price for a treat. Don't you think?"

No response except for the addition of a quivering lip. If the puppy-dog eyes didn't seal the deal, the quivering lip always did. Never let it be said that Jan didn't know how to sell a deal.

"All right, uncle. I give up," Mom said. "But only this one time. No more. Got it?"

The serious-mom eyes were out and functioning just as well as puppy-dog ones.

"Got it," Jan and Renee chorused.

Mom handed over the package of dried beef and vegetable jars, and off they went. Jan may never become an advertising executive—the whole idea of selling people things they didn't need or want seemed silly now—but nothing would stop her from becoming the best bargainer at the auction. And someday, she'd use her artistic skills to create something people would value as much as food.

«»

On the way home, Jan crammed next to Renee in the truck bed, slowly chewing on their taffy. Once the sorghum seller saw the dried beef, it cemented the sale. Jan hadn't even needed her renowned skills.

The truck jostled over something, and she almost yelped as she bumped against Renee. As she righted herself, glad to have avoided the gooseneck Dad installed to pull the cattle trailer, Caleb gave her a look she'd have stuck her tongue out at if she didn't have candy. Only two years her senior, her brother acted much older and had already resumed his serious expression, blue eyes looking nowhere as if lost in thought. His muscular body, hardened from long hours helping Dad, and handsome features along with Mom's dark hair had young women at the market turning heads. He was always there when she needed him.

With the long folding table behind their backs, she and Renee leaned on it now. Tucked in between them were the remaining unsold items and those things they'd taken in on trade. After such a busy day, not a scrap of the dried beef returned with them.

Mrs. Boswell had made an admirable trade, scoring two-dozen empty canning jars, all with the reusable lids in exchange for only one jar of spinach. Normally, an empty jar was part of the sale price for a full jar of produce, but one rarely found the reusable lids. Now the jars tinkled together as Dad slowed, while he neared potholes, to avoid breaking glass or jostling harder than they already were on the deteriorating roads. She remembered when crews kept the roads smooth as glass. Now, who knew how bad the roads would be next year?

Talked out after the day, Jan just rested her shoulder against Renee's. But it was a comfortable silence. She stretched one leg out, resting it against the back of the cab while beyond the window Renee's parents' animated gestures in the Ram's rear seat seemed to fill the silence even if Jan couldn't hear what they were saying.

Though it was hot, the wind fluttered the length of her ponytail behind her.

The truck slowed at their long driveway. This was the worst part of the ride. Dad hit the end of the driveway where a pothole had developed between the road pavement and the dirt drive. The resulting smack flung their bodies up, then back down—hard.

"Oomph."

About halfway up the driveway, the trees opened to expose their one-hundred-acre Angus beef farm, and a warm feeling of belonging enveloped her.

Once Dad had parked, they disentangled themselves from the cargo and tumbled over the side, since the tongue of the empty trailer prevented their exit via the tailgate.

"Don't leave without taking an armload, ladies." Dad reached in and handed her and Renee each a case of the empty jars. He was always efficient, rarely having to repeat any motions as he worked.

Hugging her case to her chest, Jan smirked. He had to be the most handsome man in the world with a military cut that barely allowed his graying hair to show. At six five, he projected authority without trying.

The smell of the country surrounded them. Cow patties, freshly turned soil, and wildflowers blooming somewhere close, all combined to welcome her home. Heaven.

"Mom, can the Boswells stay for supper?" she asked as her mom stepped through the door in front of her.

"Of course. Let me ask them," Mom responded.

It wouldn't be a fancy dinner, but Jan often worried her friend's family didn't have enough to eat. Mr. Boswell had taken on odd jobs since the store where he worked shut down. The variant Upsilon finished the store off right as it killed billions and caused the world supply chain to splinter irreparably.

The Boswells all appeared thinner than normal today, and Renee had ogled the dried beef they'd traded. Jan cringed. She should've given her friend the beef instead of wasting it on the treats.

After two more trips, along with everyone else, they'd carried everything into the house and followed Mom into the kitchen, the hardwood floors and marble counters cool after the heat outside. Back before the variant, Mom had let Jan help her select the new cabinets and barstools when they modernized the room. Mom had praised her artistic eye, and Jan still savored stepping into the room with its soothing matte blue and subtle recessed lighting.

"Why don't you ladies peel potatoes?" Mom asked.

"Yes, ma'am," Jan responded. When she opened the pantry, only one potato remained. "Guess we're going into the cellar."

She led Renee back outside and around the house to the root cellar door, the windowless, solid cement room creepy even with the dim light she flicked on. Never one to linger down here, she scooted across the room right quick, Renee crowding close.

"Wow." Renee shook open the bag to fill. "That potato bin's a lot lower than last time."

"It's still about a quarter full." Jan flicked away a greedy spider slinking into the bin. "It'll get us through until the fall harvest. But, seriously, let's hurry."

Together they gathered a bag full and toted them back to the kitchen. Jan's family was blessed. Her parents had installed solar panels before the shortages had begun. Back then, they had two large freezers to store their beef. That, combined with frequent power outages in the small town, led them to go solar. A freezer of spoiled meat was such a waste.

Since the outages were common and sometimes lasted for days, theirs was one of the few farms functioning without a hiccup. Having an electric stove, dishwasher, and even air conditioning was living high on the hog these days.

While the men finished evening chores, the four ladies worked in the kitchen. Then Jan headed out to the front porch and rang the dinner bell. No matter where someone was on the farm, they'd hear the bell ring. No one was late for dinner after the bell got rung.

"Set the table, please, ladies," Mom said.

Once everyone sat, she asked for a blessing on the food. "Father, we thank you for another successful day at the market. We also thank you for our dear friends who make each day serving you more joyful. Thank you for this food you give us. Amen."

Amens chorused around the table.

Soon, silverware clacked against plates and serving dishes. The scent of mashed potatoes mingled with the savory beef roast. They rarely enjoyed an entire beef roast. Instead, meat became a flavoring for vegetables and grains because it was so valuable for trade.

Mom must have noticed the weight her neighbors were losing as well. She'd be too polite to say anything, though.

Near the end of the meal, Mr. Boswell tinkled his spoon against his glass. The sound silenced all ongoing discussions. "I've got an announcement to make," he began. "We're going to be moving next week. We're heading to Columbus to look for work."

Jan's stomach fell as if on an express elevator to the basement. "What?" she shrieked. "No! You can't leave. Why can't you find work here?"

"Jan." Dad had The Look on his face. There was no argument after it arrived.

She shut her mouth and her eyes as if not seeing would stop

the inevitable. Under the table, she clenched her hands into fists, but there was no physical enemy to fight. She'd been afraid this was coming for weeks now. So many had left the town, looking for better fortunes or at least government support in the larger cities. Market day was becoming sparser each week.

Renee had been her BFF for as long as she could remember. They'd worn a path down between their two houses. Dad had even put gates in the fences so they wouldn't try sliding under the electric wires.

How would she survive without Renee?

She grabbed a hold of her friend's hand under the table and squeezed hard. This might be the last meal where they sat together at this table. Her last friend in the area was going to leave, and she couldn't do anything about it. She hated the changes the wretched variant caused to her world, the things it had stolen from her. These last years, she'd tried so hard to put on a smile, to cheer everyone up. But no pep rally could cheer her through this.

Tears rolled down her cheeks, and when she opened her eyes, she wasn't alone in shedding them.

The End

Dear reader, thank you so much for sharing Lizzy's journey with me! If you enjoyed reading *Downfall, a prequel to the Collapse Series*, I would gratefully appreciate you leaving a review on Bookbub, Goodreads, or Amazon to help others to discover my books. Those few minutes of your time make a tremendous difference to writers like me, not only in helping others find our books but also in encouraging us to keep up the effort of writing.

And with that thought, I hope you will enjoy Jan's story, the next tale in this series, *Collapse: The Death of Friendship.*

I'd love to have you join *my* posse of friends! Join my newsletter at www.AngelaDShelton.com and get the latest release information and opportunities for free books. You can also connect with me on Facebook, Instagram, Medium, and Pinterest.

See you next time! Angela